Amish Amnesia

Stephanie Swift

Published by Trellis Publishing, 2021.

AMISH AMNESIA

First edition. July 2, 2021.

Copyright © 2021 Stephanie Swift.

ISBN: 979-8224795710

Written by Stephanie Swift.

AMISH AMNESIA

STEPHANIE SWIFT

Mark Fisher stared out the hospital window and expelled a long, weary sigh. Every muscle in his body ached from the events of the past two days, and he wished for the millionth time he had someone to talk to. While his fiancé, Mary, lay sleeping in the hospital bed behind him, the beeping of her blood pressure monitor was the only thing keeping him company, and he looked anxiously toward the door, silently willing someone – even a doctor or nurse – to enter.

His parents, Mary's family, and Bishop Owen visited with them most of the day, but they had long since returned home, and part of him envied the smiling throng of people milling about on the sidewalk outside his window. It was nearing Christmas Day, and the stores across the street were decorated with a multitude of colored lights while the lampposts lining the street were clad with wreaths bedecked in holly and red ribbons. If it were any other normal day, the scene would've made him smile.

But today wasn't an ordinary day.

After Mary's carriage accident two days prior, which left her with a broken arm, two broken ribs, a concussion, and what her doctor called "temporary amnesia", their lives were turned upside down. The romantic proposal he'd rehearsed for two months, which was flawlessly executed just two weeks before, was now reduced to nothing. Mary could barely remember his name, and although the doctor assured them her memory would return, his heart ached each time she looked at him with confusion in her beautiful hazel eyes.

"Tell me again how we met."

When her soft voice interrupted the stillness, Mark walked over to her bedside. She pushed a button on the railing that would raise the bed into a sitting position, and he fluffed her pillow before sitting in the leather chair next to her bed. Although she tried to hide it, he caught the way she winced when she shifted her weight and tried to get comfortable.

He'd told her this story twice since their arrival at the hospital, but he'd happily tell her a million times if it would spark a memory – *any* memory.

"We grew up together in a little Amish town on the outside of Lancaster," he began. "You didn't care for me very much when we were younger, and you said I used to pull your hair a lot while we were in school, but I don't remember that. I think you had me confused with Thomas Troyer. He had a crush on you when we were kids too, but I was the one who won your heart."

He winked at her, and she blushed before looking down at the cast on her left arm. Her blonde hair cascaded over her shoulders, and he stopped himself from tucking it behind her ear, like he'd done numerous times before, because he didn't want to frighten her. Mark had to constantly remind himself they were starting over from scratch, despite the fact they'd known each other for twenty years and were now engaged.

"And...and we're supposed to be getting married soon?" she asked.

He detected the hesitancy in her voice, and he swallowed hard past the lump in his throat. She furrowed a brow at him, but he saw no recollection in her gaze. She still looked upon him like she would a stranger – with caution and trepidation. It broke his heart, but he was determined to remain positive and help her find her way back, no matter how long it took.

"I proposed to you a couple of weeks ago, and you said yes. We talked about having a spring wedding, but there's no rush. Let's just take this one day at a time and focus on getting you well."

He reached out and lightly grasped her hand, and he was relieved when she didn't jerk away from him, like she did the first time she opened her eyes and saw him in the emergency room, immediately following the accident. Remembering the terrified look on her face made his heart ache, but she'd come a long way in just two days. At least now she didn't seem as frightened by his presence.

"Can you please tell me about the accident again?" she asked.

Mark scooted to the edge of his chair and propped his elbows on the hospital bed.

"You were on your way to Lancaster when a teenager ran a stop sign as you turned on to the main road. Fortunately, he wasn't going very fast, but his car forced the carriage off the road and into a ditch. You hit your head, and you were unconscious until you arrived at the hospital in the ambulance. Princess is a little banged up, but she's going to be fine."

Mary squinted. "Princess?"

Mark caressed the back of her hand and smiled. "Your horse – the one pulling the carriage. You've had her since you were twelve years old."

His comment seemed to ignite a tiny bit of recognition in her eyes, and she nodded before resting her head on the pillow. "That's good. I'm glad she's okay."

He could tell she was getting sleepy again, and even though he wanted more than anything to keep her awake and talk to her longer, he knew she needed to rest.

"The doctor said you should be able to go home tomorrow morning," he said. "Everyone there is anxious to see you."

She gave him another weary smile, and within a matter of seconds she was sound asleep. Mark gently kissed her hand before releasing it and easing back in his chair. He wanted to rest too, but at the moment there were too many things plaguing his heart and mind.

"*Gott*, please bring her back to me," he whispered.

Mark leaned his head against the chair and closed his eyes. Although their friends and neighbors were well aware of the situation and Mary's amnesia, he couldn't help but worry over what might be said and done once she returned home. The doctor suggested several times taking things slowly, and even though they meant no harm, he worried their community might try to rush her and pull her even farther from his grasp.

Mark sighed as he soothed his mind by counting the steady beeps of Mary's blood pressure monitor, which eventually lulled him to sleep.

* * * *

Mary took Mark's hand and slowly stepped out of the taxi the following morning. She felt a bit queasy after the long ride home from the hospital, but she forced a smile when she saw the horde of people waiting for her on her parents' front porch.

While the taxi driver and Mark retrieved her suitcase from the trunk, she cautiously inched her way toward the house. Her parents bolted down the steps and rushed to her side to help, and although she was extremely grateful for their concern, she secretly wished everyone would stop coddling her.

"Let's get you inside so you can rest," her *Mamm* suggested. "The women have been busy preparing meals, and there's so much food in our refrigerator I probably won't have to cook for a month."

She laughed when she said it, and Mary tried to share in her excitement, but as nausea wreaked havoc with her insides, the last thing she wanted to think about was food.

As her doctor reassured her from the beginning, Mary's memory was returning in bits and pieces. She easily recalled the names of every person on her porch, and when her *Daed* opened the front door, Mary went straight to the left side of the living room sofa, after remembering there were loose springs under the cushion on the right side that squeaked like an ornery pig every time someone sat there.

The pain in her ribs and arm didn't help with the nausea, but she did her best to maintain a smile while talking to her visitors. As soon as they all left, however, she allowed her pent-up tears to fall. She wasn't used to feeling so helpless and frustrated, and she didn't like it – not one bit.

"Oh, sweetie. What can I do?" her *Mamm* asked. "Are you hurting? Do you need to lie down?"

Mark left the kitchen and joined them as soon as he overheard their conversation, and she hastily wiped the tears away so he wouldn't worry. Although most of her memories had returned, there were still holes were Mark was concerned, but there was no mistaking the way her heartbeat escalated when he was near. He'd faithfully remained by her side while she was in the hospital, and he was more patient with her incessant questions than most people would have been. With his help, she was able to fill in some of the gaps, but she still couldn't recall much about their courtship.

Mary shook her head and squeezed her *Mamm's* hand. "I'm just feeling a bit overwhelmed right now, but I'll be okay. Is Princess in the barn? I'd like to check on her."

Mark nodded. "I'll take you to see her."

He and her *Mamm* helped her stand, and after a couple of wobbly steps, she carefully made her way through the hall and out the back door of the house. Mark kept a firm grip on her during their short walk to the barn, and she felt her cheeks flush as the heat from his touch warmed her skin and gave her goosebumps.

"I hate feeling so helpless," she admitted.

Mark chuckled at her remark as he slid the barn door open so she could enter.

"You've never been helpless a day in your life, Mary. You're way too stubborn to let anything keep you down for long. I promise you'll be feeling like your old self in no time."

His comment made her smile, and his positive outlook was reassuring and helped to renew her waning faith.

"You make it sound like I'm quite the handful," she teased.

Mark wrapped his arm around her waist and guided her to a far corner of the barn, where Princess was busy munching on some hay in one of the stalls.

"You can be, sometimes, but you've called me hardheaded on more than one occasion, so I guess we have that in common."

His playful remark made a rush of heat course through her veins, and she turned her attention to Princess to avoid looking in his eyes. The horse ambled her way over as soon as she spotted them, and when she nuzzled her snout against her face, Mary gave her an affectionate rub along her neck, which made her whinny loudly in response.

"She's missed you," Mark said.

Her mind filled with a quick burst of memories, from riding Princess in the field behind her house when she was younger, to the numerous times Princess pulled the carriage on her trips into Lancaster. Mary glanced over Princess' body, and she frowned when she noticed the shallow cuts on her legs and right side.

"I hate so much this happened to her," Mary said. "It's a miracle she wasn't killed."

Mark grasped her hand and turned her around to face him. "*You* are a miracle too. I...I don't know what I would've done if *Gott* had decided to take you home. I can't bear to think about it."

Mary didn't know how to respond. The corners of his eyes filled with tears, and he looked visibly distraught. Even though she was still trapped inside her own mind when it came to him and their relationship, she felt inexplicitly drawn to Mark, and when Mary reached out and gently traced his jawline with her fingertips, she could tell the gesture caught him by surprise.

Her heart thumped erratically when he leaned in to kiss her, and although her cautious nature warned her to stop moving so quickly, the curious side of her eventually won. His lips were soft and warm against her own, and her whole body flooded with a peaceful reassurance as soon as their lips touched. Mark deepened their kiss, and she couldn't deny it felt wonderful and right being in his arms.

"I love you so much, Mary."

She wished she could tell him she loved him too, but nothing could change the fact he was practically a stranger – at least in her mind. She hoped and prayed *Gott* would restore all of her memories, but she had to face the fact there was a chance He might not, and she couldn't lead Mark on and give him false hope.

He attempted to kiss her again, but Princess whinnied and startled them both, and Mary laughed softly as she looked down at her feet so Mark wouldn't notice her flushed cheeks.

"I think someone is jealous I'm getting all the attention," he whispered.

Mary nodded as she ran her hand along Princess' mane to soothe her. "I should probably get back inside. It's late, and I'm feeling a bit tired."

Mark agreed, and after giving Princess a few more strokes along her neck, she closed the stall gate and let Mark help her back to the house. She took slow, cautious steps, trying to prolong their walk so she could feel his strong arm holding her as long as possible.

"Have you been able to recall any details about the accident?" he asked.

She gave him a curious look before shaking her head. "Unfortunately, no. All I remember is hitching my carriage for the trip to Lancaster and then waking up in the emergency room."

He didn't reply, and as they eased up the back-porch steps and walked inside the house, the scent of freshly brewed coffee drifted down the hallway and made her mouth water. Before they joined her parents in the kitchen, Mark pulled her close and gave her one last brief kiss on the lips.

* * * *

Mark frowned as he removed a familiar beige envelope from his mailbox and turned it over in his hand. As he suspected, it was addressed from his uncle William, who lived in Dayton, Ohio.

Christmas had come and gone, and he'd spent most of it working at his future in-law's sawmill and spending as much time as possible with Mary.

She'd made a great deal of progress since her hospital stay, and although she still couldn't remember some of the more prominent details about their life together, he had faith that *Gott* would completely restore her in His own time.

Mark stuffed the envelope in his coat pocket and carried the rest of his mail to his house, where he tossed it on the kitchen table before sitting down and cradling his head in his hands. He didn't have to read the letter to know what it would say. Before Mary's accident, he'd been corresponding regularly with his uncle William and aunt Paula about moving to Dayton after the wedding and taking over management of his dairy farm, since the two of them were in ill health and had no children of their own to care for the business.

He was more than ready to pack his belongings and move, but Mary was adamantly against leaving her family. The last time they'd discussed it was the morning of her accident, and he groaned out loud when he recalled the huge argument that ensued as soon as he mentioned it. Mark removed the envelope from his pocket and opened it, and as he slid the letter from its confines, he took a deep breath before reading it.

Dear nephew,

We hope this finds you well, and we pray your Christmas was a blessed one. We were concerned when we didn't hear from you before the holiday, but we know how busy you've been with work and Mary. Have you had the chance to speak with her about moving to Dayton? If so, we hope she agreed because there's no one we'd rather leave our business with than the two of you. We will completely understand, though, if you decide against it, but we hope you'll consider visiting us before the wedding so you can see for yourself what a profitable business it would be for you and your (future) family. We love you and look forward to hearing from you again soon.

Love,

Uncle William and aunt Paula

Before he had the chance to contemplate what he'd read, there was a knock on his front door, and Mark hurriedly shoved the letter inside the envelope before hiding it in one of the kitchen drawers. He really wasn't in the mood for company, and he hoped whoever was visiting didn't plan on staying long, but his dread turned to happiness when he opened the door and found Mary standing on his threshold.

"I remembered our first date!" she exclaimed, with a big smile adorning her beautiful face.

Before he had the opportunity to reply, she walked past him and into the living room, all the while talking excitedly about the first picnic they shared many months prior.

"It was a Saturday afternoon, and you came to my house and asked my *Daed* for permission to escort me to the lake for a picnic," she explained. "You brought a wicker basket packed with two sandwiches, a mason jar full of lemonade, and something else...what was it? Oh! It was two slices of your *Mamm's* apple pie!"

It was endearing seeing her so ecstatic over the recollection of their first date, and the memory brought a smile to his face too.

"*Yah*...you're right," he replied. "I also brought a poem I'd written for you."

Mary's cheeks reddened as she reached inside a pocket of her dress and pulled out a piece of paper that was worn and tattered on the edges.

"*Yah*. I remembered where I keep in hidden in my bedroom too. I've read it so many times I could probably recite it by memory."

He took the paper from her hand and carefully unfolded it. The ink had faded, but he could still recall the angst he endured after spending nearly two weeks writing it. Finding out she'd kept it this whole time made his heart swell.

"Ever since I woke up this morning I've been bombarded with so many memories. It's like a floodgate finally opened, and I'm slowly but surely getting my life back."

She anxiously paced the floor while she talked, and she was so elated he didn't want to do anything that might spoil her mood – namely bringing their recent argument to light. That was one memory she evidently hadn't recalled yet and realizing she could do so at any time made his insides churn. He contemplated showing her the letter from his aunt and uncle, but he just couldn't bring himself to ruin the moment.

"Do you remember what else happened that day?" he asked.

Mary stopped moving and turned to him with a sly grin on her face. When she closed the small gap between them and placed a hand over his heart, the faint scent of her lavender lotion wafted past his nose and made his pulse race.

"We shared our first kiss," she said. "After we ate lunch, you took me by the hand, and we went for a stroll around the lake. I was so nervous, but when you kissed me, I knew I was right where I was meant to be, and that nervousness just melted away."

She stood on her tiptoes and tenderly kissed his lips, and he gripped her waist and held her tight against his body. The cast and sling on her arm kept him from holding her as close as he wanted to, but he was careful not to hurt her.

"Are you feeling better?" he asked, while tucking a stray strand of hair behind her ear and sliding his fingertips gently down the side of her neck, which made her quiver in response.

"*Yah*. I was finally able to get a good night's rest last night, and I believe that helped a lot. I'm starting to get cabin fever though. Can we get away from here for a little while? Maybe go for a walk around the lake or take a short trip into Lancaster?"

Mark kissed her forehead before releasing her. "That sounds like a good idea to me. I need to pick up some supplies at the hardware store anyway."

Mary bounced up and down excitedly, and as Mark retrieved his hat from the wooden hanger beside his front door, he pushed his worries far from his mind so he could enjoy the day with his bride-to-be.

* * * *

Mary sat straight up in bed the following morning and immediately wished she hadn't moved so quickly as a strong surge of pain radiated through her ribs and made her nauseous. She'd been sleeping peacefully when flashbacks from her accident began coursing through her mind at an alarming pace and woke her in an instant. As her heart pounded furiously inside her chest, she took a couple of deep breaths to try and steady her breathing, but nothing could quell the confusing thoughts that consumed her.

The sun was starting to rise in the east, and as the bright rays streamed through her bedroom window, she carefully stood and walked to the closet. She had questions, and the only one who could answer them was Mark. He'd told her repeatedly that the accident was caused by a teenager running a stop sign, but her flashbacks were telling her differently.

A knock on her bedroom door stole her from her reverie, and as her *Mamm* opened it and stuck her head inside, she attempted a smile that she hoped was believable.

"*Guder mariye*," Mary said.

Her *Mamm* walked in the room and placed a steaming cup of coffee on her dresser.

"I thought I heard you stirring around in here. What are you doing up so early?" her *Mamm* asked.

Mary pulled a blue dress and white apron from her closet and laid them at the foot of the bed before sitting down.

"I'm not sure. I guess all this rest is starting to get the best of me, and I'm just anxious to move around a bit," she replied.

She hated lying to her, but until she talked to Mark, she figured it would be best to keep her worries to herself.

"Well, don't get too carried away. You need to take care of yourself and give your body time to heal. Everything else can wait."

Mary forced a smile and nodded.

"Breakfast will be ready in a few minutes, if you'd like to join us. I know you haven't been very hungry the past few days, but you need to keep your strength up."

Again, Mary smiled and agreed. When her *Mamm* turned and left her bedroom, she sighed with relief before changing clothes, which took much longer than usual with the cast on her arm and the gauze bandages cinching her ribcage. By the time she finished, she felt as if she'd been in a race, but she did manage to work up an appetite.

After brushing her teeth and combing her hair, Mary joined her parents in the kitchen for breakfast. They were busy talking about the upcoming church festival, and she was thankful they had a subject to keep them occupied, since she had other things on her mind and wanted to be left alone with her thoughts.

She was midway into her meal when Mark showed up for work, and as soon as he walked in the front door, she stood and put her plate away so she could spend a few minutes with him before he and her *Daed* left for the sawmill.

"*Guder mariye*, Mark," her *Mamm* called. "There's plenty of eggs and bacon left if you would like eat breakfast with us."

Mark took off his hat and smiled. "*Denki*, Mrs. Miller, but I ate before I left the house this morning. Perhaps some other time."

Mary decided to intervene before her parents pulled him into some lengthy conversation that would ruin her chances of speaking to him alone.

"Let's go for a walk while *Daed* finishes eating. I could use the exercise," she suggested.

Mark gave her a quizzical look, but he didn't object, and as they left the kitchen and made their way out the back door, she mulled over in her mind the best way to approach him about the flashbacks that jarred her awake.

Mark held her hand as they walked to the fence surrounding the corn field behind her house, and her knees felt wobbly as the heat from his skin warmed her body and made her swoon.

"Is something wrong?" he asked. "You seemed pretty anxious to get away from your folks."

Mary gazed over the field, where the tall corn stalks swayed and bent with the breeze and considered leaving the subject alone. For all she knew, it could've been just a bad dream and not her memories trying to resurface. She hated to make something out of nothing.

Mark put his arm around her waist and held her close, and she took a deep breath before attempting to speak, knowing if she didn't talk about it the uncertainty would bother her even more.

"I had the strangest dream last night," she began. "In the dream, you and I were walking home from church, and we got into a terrible argument, but I can't remember what it was about. We parted ways – well, actually, I stormed off and left you behind."

Mark removed his arm from her waist and leaned against the wooden fence. He turned his attention to the field and wouldn't look at her, and the atmosphere changed immediately, which made the tiny hairs on the back of her neck stand up.

"I came home and hitched Princess to the carriage so I could take the quilts I'd made to Mrs. Holloway's store in Lancaster. They weren't due until the next day, but for some reason I just wanted to get away for a while. I was upset during the ride, and I remember very vividly that I was crying. I came to the four-way stop at the end of the main road, and...I woke up."

Mark cleared his throat before looking down at the ground and digging the heel of his left boot into the dirt. She could tell something was on his mind, and she remained quiet, to give him the chance to share what he was thinking about, but several minutes passed, and he never said a word.

"Honestly, I'm not sure if it was a dream or if they were memories trying to resurface, but either way, it has me worried. If I was upset the day of my accident, there's a chance it was my fault. I could've been distracted and..."

Mark vehemently shook his head. "*Neh*. That's not what happened. The sheriff investigated it, and the teenager driving the car admitted he was texting on his cell phone and ran the stop sign. It wasn't your fault. Don't even think that way."

Mary felt somewhat reassured, but there were still other questions that needed answering.

"So, it was just a bad dream then, and we weren't fighting," she replied, trying not to sound as desperately hopeful as she felt.

Mark moved away from the fence and slid his hands inside his coat pockets. When he finally looked at her, she could tell right away that something was wrong, which made her heart plummet to her feet.

"Mark? Is there something you need to tell me?"

He closed his eyes and tilted his head toward the sun, and when he opened them again she could see the faintest glimmer of tears hiding in the corners.

"We did argue that morning," he admitted. "It was the first time we'd ever disagreed on something, and it became very heated very fast. When you walked away from me, I honestly thought we were through."

Mary tilted her head and gave him a curious look.

"Mark, when I accepted your proposal, I made a promise before *Gott* that I would always love you and stand by you. I don't understand what could've been so bad that it almost caused us to break up. Is...is there someone else?"

Mark's gaze widened as he closed the distance between them and tenderly cradled her head in his hands. "Of course not. I would never do that to you, Mary. There's no one else I'd rather spend the rest of my life with than you."

His sweet words made her smile, but it did nothing to end her confusion.

"We were arguing because...because I told you I wanted to move to Dayton and take over my uncle William's dairy business after we got married."

Mary took a step back. Instantly, her mind drifted to her parents, her older brother, and the other family members who lived in the community. Not to mention, the countless friends she'd grown up with. The farthest she'd been away from home was during her hospital stay in Lancaster, and just the thought of moving to another state made her pulse quicken.

"Why would you want to move when our whole life is right here?" she asked.

Mark went back to the fence and braced himself against it. For the longest while, he never spoke, and with each passing minute, Mary felt her anxiety increase more and more.

"Your *Daed's* sawmill will never be mine, Mary. You know as well as I do that he will hand the business to your brother someday. My uncle William and aunt Paula have no children, and they want to pass their dairy business along to me – to *us*. We could build a house there and raise a family, and we would be set for the rest of our lives."

Mary couldn't believe what she was hearing. Of all the possibilities that raced through her mind that morning over what her dream could've been about, she'd never once imagined it had anything to do with leaving her home.

"But what about our family and my quilting business? The only people we know in Dayton are your aunt and uncle."

She could feel her temper bristle the more she thought about having to pack up her life and move away from everyone and everything she knew and cared so much about.

"Mary, we could build a life together in Dayton."

The squeaking of rusty hinges caught her attention, and she looked toward the house just as her *Daed* exited through the back door and began making his way to the sawmill inside his barn.

"We could build a life together *here* just as easily as we could in Ohio," she replied.

Her words came out sounding harsher than she expected, but she couldn't control the anger and resentment boiling inside her, and Mary walked away before she said something she truly regretted.

* * * *

Mark turned the envelope over and over again in his hands before placing a stamp on it and forcing himself to move from the kitchen table to the front door. After a sleepless night spent tossing and turning and mulling over the pros and cons repeatedly, he'd come to a decision that he felt would not only benefit himself but Mary too.

As he bounded down his front porch steps and strode to the mailbox, he felt more at peace than he had in weeks, and he said a silent prayer of thanks to *Gott* for pointing him in the right direction. He knew some people wouldn't be happy with his choice, but he was a grown man capable of making his own path in life, and that kept his shoulders back and his head held high.

"Mark?"

The sound of Mary's voice was like a soothing balm, especially after the uncomfortable silence between them following their disagreement the day before. When he turned around to face her, he was caught off guard when she practically leapt at him and hugged him tight. Mark encircled her waist and enjoyed the moment and the way her soft body melded so perfectly to his own.

"I'm sorry," she whispered.

Mark smiled. "You have nothing to apologize for. I was the one who sprang this on you without considering your feelings."

Mary took his hand and led him to his front porch steps so they could sit down.

"I've spent a lot of time thinking about what you said," she replied. "And if this is something you feel strongly about, then we should do it. I know you only want what's best for our future, and I love you for that."

Mark held up a hand to stop her.

"Actually...I think it would be best if we stayed here."

She leaned back and gave him a curious look, which made him smile.

"I've been thinking a lot about what you said too, and you were right. We need our family and friends. Witnessing how they took care of you after your accident made that even more clear to me. *Yah*, I would love to have my own business someday, but that's not as important to me as your happiness."

Mary kissed his cheek.

"You know, we could always start our own business," she suggested. "There's no rule that says you have to work at my *Daed's* sawmill forever, and no one else here has a dairy farm, so it would be a good investment. It would also be a great thing to share with our children...someday."

The thought made him grin from ear to ear, and it also filled him with hope.

"But what about your uncle William and aunt Paula? Will they understand?"

Mark looked up at the clouds and hugged her close to his body.

"I wrote them a letter and explained our situation. I'm sure they'll be disappointed at first, but they have other options, so I feel certain they will be okay. I would like to visit them soon, though, just to make sure they leave their business in the right hands."

Mary nodded. "I understand, and I'd like to go with you too. Maybe we can plan a trip once my arm and ribs are completely healed."

Mark stood and held out a hand to help her up. "That sounds like a good idea to me. Now, let's go inside and eat some peach pie. I'm starving."

Mary laughed as they made their way to the front door. "Did your *Mamm* bake one for you?"

Mark flashed her a mischievous smile as they walked inside. "*Neh*, believe it or not, I baked it myself. It might not be fit to eat, but I couldn't sleep last night, so I decided to do something constructive."

Mary looked visibly impressed. "Why, Mark Fisher…you're just full of surprises today. Maybe we should argue more often and see if we can't turn you into a chef."

Mark threw his head back and laughed before walking to the kitchen cabinet and retrieving two plates and a couple of forks. "No way, no how. I don't like it when we fight."

Mary gave him a quick kiss on the lips. "I don't like it either…but I could get used to this making up part."

Mark grinned as he leaned in and returned her kiss, but he took his time and drew it out, deepening the kiss to the point where they were both left breathless when they parted.

He removed the pie from the oven and brought two pieces of it back to the table, where they sat down across from each other and said grace before digging in. As Mary brought a forkful to her mouth, Mark held his breath and waited expectantly for her reaction. She closed her eyes and chewed it slowly, but it wasn't long before she looked his way and gave him a approving nod.

"Not bad," she said. "Not bad at all."

Mark's heart raced as he admired the way her hazel eyes sparkled when she talked and the sultry curve of her lips when she smiled. He knew, without a doubt in his mind, that he was one very lucky man.

"I couldn't agree with you more."

Tears of an Amish Widow

Erica Hennig

There were a lot of things in life that Hannah King imagined she'd be. A mother, a wife, possibly even a mentor to young women; a widow was not something she'd imagined for herself.

There was an illness running through the little Plain community. It was something like pneumonia, but the English doctors were having a hard time controlling it as well. Hannah's husband, Joab, was a farmer with a caring heart. He chose to follow the doctor around and help him however he could. Since the illness was contagious, Joab eventually became sick.

Hannah wasn't going to let this illness stay in the community anymore. She made the decision to take Joab to the actual English hospital. Though they were able to keep him alive a little longer, they still could not save Joab. Hannah was crushed, her heart felt as though it had been ripped out of her chest and beaten with a sledgehammer over and over.

How am I going to take care of our little Samuel? How will I live? Who will take care of me?

The oncoming depression wasn't one she could push away with a few good thoughts and a well-placed Bible verse. She desperately tried praying, hoping that the God she served would send a sign that everything would be alright... but nothing came. No signs in the sky, no angels to comfort, and no one to care for her and her little boy.

Ultimately, she knew that the community would take care of her for a time, but she also knew that she would have to pull herself together eventually. Especially if she was going to continue to support her son. He no longer had a father, and Hannah was determined to make sure he had a mother.

Day in and day out, she began to do what she could to care for Samuel. She worked in the local store, and sold things she knitted at the market on the weekends. Hannah would help in the schoolhouse if they let her, and they did until Samuel got to be the age that he could go to school. The community leaders decided having one of the students' parents there would cause a conflict in the community as to why a certain parent was allowed there and none others.

Just as the new school year was around the corner, the school teacher—Miss Schwartz—got married and decided to quit teaching. Hannah didn't understand how the community could let something like that happen. She went on a rampage one day and told the leaders exactly what she thought of them in the little church building where they were meeting.

"How could you leave the children with no one? Who in this community will train our children on the right path? You must have *something* in place! Surely, you're not that stupid."

She heard a throat clear behind her and saw a handsome, young man standing in the doorway. He smiled as her face flushed with embarrassment.

"Ms. King, this is Michael Fisher," one of the elders said. "He will be the new school teacher. We have decided that you will assist him for the first three weeks of classes, then you must find something else to occupy your time."

"'Occupy my time?' You make teaching sound like a hobby! Isn't investing in the next generation important to you?" Hannah felt a hand on her shoulder and she knew it was the new guy, Michael. Something about his touch calmed her, and her heart instantly ached for the tender touch of a husband again.

"Ms. King," Michael's voice was barely above a whisper. "Let them do what they feel is right. I care about the children just as much as you do. We'll work something out for you."

Hannah relaxed a little, nodded in response, then turned around and walked out of the church. She discovered that the men in that room might not have cared for the children, but the man taking over as school teacher certainly did. And she could get behind a man that was confident in what he was doing. She was going to make the next three weeks the most meaningful yet.

Samuel was so excited for the first day of school that he could hardly contain himself. Hannah walked with him a little earlier than most other students. She wanted to be there early to make a better impression than the first time for Michael.

He probably won't even remember me anyway, she thought to herself. *Almost every single girl in the community has made contact with him. I'm sure we've all started to look the same to him.* Though Hannah was afraid to admit what exactly that meant, even to herself. She hated lumping herself in with all of the young, unmarried girls in the community, but sometimes she found herself acting just like them. Of course it was only a few years ago that she was unmarried and pining for every guy that walked into her life.

Her train of thought was interrupted by Samuel suddenly dashing off toward the school.

"Samuel, wait!"

Hannah tried to call him back or catch up with him, but he had such a head start that he was in the school building before she had even crested the hill the school was standing on. Michael popped his head out of the door, probably looking for the parents of the small child who had just entered the school an entire hour before school was even to start. As soon as he saw Hannah, he smiled wide.

"Ms. King," he declared instantly.

So much for forgetting who I am, she thought as her face grew warm.

"Mr. Fisher," she spoke politely. "I just want to apologize for the way we met—"

Michael held his hand up. "No need. All is forgiven. And please, call me Michael."

"Hannah." She stuck out her hand for him to shake, but he took it and kissed it lightly instead. Her heart skipped a beat.

"The pleasure is mine," he said as he looked into her eyes. His were a deep green that fit well with the sandy blond hair on his head and tan skin she could see. Hannah thought he looked almost too tan to be a teacher, but decided the first official meeting wasn't the right time to bring that up.

"Samuel and I are here early to help you set up since it's the first day of school," Hannah quickly changed the subject before her mind went any further away from the original reason she was there so early.

Michael turned and walked into the building, ready to have a helper there.

"I'm glad you'll be here for a few weeks. Sometimes the first three weeks are the hardest on a teacher."

"You've taught before?" Samuel sounded surprised. Michael laughed.

"Of course, buddy," Michael bent down to Samuel's level and addressed him directly. "I was a teacher in another community before I came here."

"Why didn't you stay there then?"

"Because I heard there was another town that needed help, and I like a good hero story." Michael winked as Samuel's eyes grew wide.

Hannah laughed at the exchange before telling Samuel to make sure that every desk had pencils.

As the boy ran off, Hannah began to explain to Michael what they had done last year before Michael cut her off with a wave of his hand.

"I do appreciate the input Hannah, but I would like to do something a little different this time. The children don't know me, and I don't know any of them. I don't want to really come down as an overbearing teacher on my first day." Michael winked. Hannah didn't understand that logic, and she certainly didn't appreciate feeling like she was being spoken to condescendingly.

"Excuse me, sir, but I think we should at least address what the children did." Hannah was going to let him have it anyway. "The children come here to learn, not to make friends with the teacher. If you think for one second I'll let you get away with talking to me like that, you have some life choices to reevaluate." Michael's eyebrows shot up, but he didn't say anything.

Hannah continued. "You might think you're some big hot shot coming here on the invitation of the elders, but you're only here because I already have a child and they won't let parents of a child in the school be the teacher. So you can take the smug, entitled attitude and stick it... somewhere!" She turned and walked out of the building, now feeling like a bit of a moron for telling the handsome, new school teacher off. She was only outside a few minutes before Samuel came and got her.

"Mama, don't let Mr. Fisher scare you away," he spoke tenderly to her. "Besides, maybe he can help you become an even better hero." Hannah looked at her son and realized that even though she didn't think very highly of herself, he thought the world of her. And she wasn't going to let him down; not today, and not ever.

"Okay," she consented as she gave Samuel a hug. "Let's go inside and show him how it's done."

The next few week flew by quickly, and the fact that Michael had been making subtle advances wasn't lost on Hannah. She loved the fact that someone was even toying with the idea of courting her. Since it had been almost five years since Joab had passed on, Hannah didn't think any man would ever take a liking to a woman with a child.

There was only a small problem with the whole situation, and Hannah hated to admit it to herself. Abigail Miller had also shown an interest in the young Mr. Fisher. She was by far the prettiest girl in town with her beautiful blonde hair, deep blue eyes and nearly flawless skin. There wasn't much wrong with Abigail, except that if she didn't get her way she tended to have a fit. But with all of the guys in town constantly pining for her, that rarely happened. Until Michael Fisher came along.

Hannah wasn't sure if he was declining young Abigail's advances or simply playing hard to get, but it made Hannah a little nervous. She felt like there might have been something between them, but this was the last day that she would see Michael on a regular basis. Since it wasn't out of the realm of normal things she would do, she had already decided that she would walk Samuel home from school everyday. Especially if that meant she got to see Michael Fisher for a few minutes.

As all of the children were released to go home, Hannah decided to see if she could get an idea of what was going on in his head.

"This is my last day," she picked up a pencil off the floor as if it was the only purpose she had in the world. She looked up at Michael at the front of the room. He simply nodded, his face tight with emotion.

"Are you okay?" Suddenly nothing else mattered. She moved to the front of the room and stood next to him.

"I just hate it that things have to come to an end," he began to cry. Hannah was shocked. She'd never really seen a grown man cry before, and she wasn't sure what to do. She put her hand on his arm.

"How can I help you?"

"You can stay," he chuckled. They both knew that wasn't her decision and she said as much. Michael replied, "That doesn't mean you can't try to get an extension."

"I'm a woman," Hannah shot back. "They are far less likely to listen to me than they are to you. Besides, you're the teacher. You know what you need far better than I do."

"All I need is you."

Hannah froze. Did she just hear him correctly? "What?"

He pulled away. "You're right, I shouldn't have said that. I apologize." He began busying himself with unnecessary papers on the desk.

"Michael." Hannah grabbed his arm and he stopped. He looked at her and their eyes met. Tears were brimming in his eyes. She wanted to hear him say it again. "What did you say?"

"All I need is you." He turned to face her fully. Her heartbeat sped up, but her breathing became shallow. She knew this feeling; Joab used to make her feel this way. But Joab was gone, so she attempted to push all thoughts of her dead husband out of her mind.

Michael looked at her a moment longer, but he must have seen the inner turmoil because he finally said, "No." And he turned and went back to the useless straightening.

"Did I do something wrong?" Hannah's heart hurt a little as she was suddenly treated very coldly. He stopped.

"No, but I need to take this slowly. Not for your sake, but for mine. There's so much I haven't been able to tell you because we've been at school. Let's have dinner tonight. Bring Samuel. The Miller's live right next door and they have a son he can play with."

Hannah knew the Miller's well, especially because Abigail was the one after Michael's heart. This was a good sign though, because it meant that although Abigail was trying, she wasn't doing as well as she might have thought. And she wasn't asked over for dinner like Hannah. She would still be careful not to give in too much to this. There had been too many times already where men thought they wanted Hannah, but they didn't want Samuel. Since the pair were a package deal, there wasn't much option once they realized how serious Hannah was about her son.

I guess we'll find out tonight how he really feels.

As he usually was, Samuel was ecstatic to be spending any time with Mr. Fisher.

"Do we need to bring anything, Mama? I can't imagine that a *man* would cook anything well." Samuel made a face as he finished his thought. Hannah laughed.

"Samuel, don't be so mean," she playfully scolded him. "Maybe he had all sisters and learned how to cook from them. Maybe he was an only child. I don't know, but you can ask him when we get there."

The ten-minute walk seemed to be the longest walk of their lives. As they got closer, Samuel got more talkative, but Hannah became more quiet. *What if he decides he doesn't like me? How will I tell Samuel?*

Does he even like Samuel? It seems as though he likes children, but sometimes Samuel is a handful. Maybe we should turn around...

The doubting game was becoming too much. Hannah felt a hand wrap around her hand and looked down to find her son had grasped her and was smiling up at her.

"Remember Mama," Samuel said sweetly. "No matter what this man thinks of you, I still love you." She felt an unchecked tear slide down her cheek. She stopped and scooped the little boy into her arms, as they held each other and cried. When Hannah finally put Samuel down he said, "Besides, Jesus still loves you too. And He's the only man you need that *really* matters."

Hannah had to keep from crying because they had already rounded the corner onto the street where Michael lived and he was standing in the doorway waiting for them. Hannah began to apologize for keeping him waiting, but he just waved his hand as he usually did when he didn't want to hear excuses.

"Anything you need to say isn't going to make up for the lost time, so let's not waste any more with apologies." He smiled as if to say there was no need to feel bad for anything she did, though she still felt the need to apologize for apologizing before realizing that would have been counterproductive. She stepped over the threshhold behind her son and was surprised to see an almost immaculate house with the smell of roast beef, carrots and potatoes wafting throughout.

"Mama, it doesn't smell this good when you cook!" Samuel seemed to suddenly have no filter. Thankfully, Michael took it gracefully and defended Hannah's honor.

"Now now, that's not what we say to our mother, is it?" He knelt to Samuel's level, ever the teacher. "She cooks for you, doesn't she?"

The little boy nodded.

"You're never hungry, are you?"

He shook his head.

"Do you sleep in a house?"

A nod.

"Do you have decent clothes to wear?"

Another nod.

"How about some nice shoes?"

One more nod for good measure.

"Then you only say nice things about the woman that treats you well."

"Yes sir," Samuel said before Michael nodded and stood.

"Now," he clapped his hands together. "Who's ready for dinner?"

During dinner, Samuel asked every question he said he was going to, from how he knows how to cook to why is his house so clean to why does he teach. Everything seemed to be going really well until suddenly the 5-year-old had a different plan for the interrogation.

"Do you plan on marrying Mama?"

Hannah's face quickly grew warm and she studied the plate in front of her, afraid of what Michael would say. *This wasn't supposed to happen!*

Without skipping a beat, Michael replied, "Well, that really depends on her. I've already made my decision, but if she keeps pushing me away... then we'll see."

"That would be really stinky. Because Mama really likes you and she's a lot happier with you in her life. In fact, I don't think I've ever seen her this happy. She even sings in her sleep now." Michael laughed at the boy's sudden burst of random facts.

"Oh, does she?" Samuel wasn't even phased.

"Yeah. I think they're songs she used to sing with Papa, but I was a baby when he died, so I only hear stories now. But I think she told me once that was a song she used to sing with him." Samuel shrugged before adding, "Do you have anything for dessert?"

"As a matter of fact I do. Then, you should go play with David Miller next door while you Mama and I talk about grown up stuff."

Samuel seemed to like that idea, so Michael went to get the dessert. Strawberry shortcake with vanilla ice cream.

"Where did you learn how to make ice cream?" Hannah tried to keep the conversation away from their relationship for the time being. She was still reeling from the question of marriage.

"Oh that's simple stuff really... I just went to the English store in town." They all laughed. "More accurately, I have a Mennonite friend who gives me ice cream on a regular basis. It's a treat for me and not one I share with everyone. Tonight, I have two honored guests in my home and I want you both to know that you're special to me."

It was quiet for a few moments, but finally Samuel pushed his chair back and got up from the table without asking.

"I think that was my cue to leave." With that, he walked out the front door and closed it behind him.

"I can't argue with his logic, even if he didn't ask to be excused." Michael looked at Hannah and began his thought. "I've been meaning to tell you this since I met you, but I really do have intentions of marrying you... but like I told Samuel, that is entirely up to you." He sighed and leaned back in his chair. "Would you like to move to the living room? The dishes can wait until later."

Hannah was so enamored by the way Michael's house looked that she couldn't imagine that he was actually fine with leaving dishes unwashed, but she didn't argue because she knew this was a conversation they needed to have.

Once they sat down and were comfortable, Michael continued his thought.

"There is no one in this world who has made me feel more comfortable than you have. From the second I heard how passionate you were about the children until I saw you and Samuel walking up to my house with red eyes from crying, and right up until this moment; there is no one in the world I want in my life more than you and Samuel." He smiled when he said her son's name.

"Who named him?" Michael asked.

"Joab did. He was sick when Samuel was born and said that I was to dedicate him to the Lord just like Hannah did in the Bible."

"Were you having trouble conceiving as well? Actually, I'm sorry—"

Hannah laughed. "No apologies needed, and no we weren't. But he knew from the start that he probably wasn't going to make it. In some ways, it made his passing easier, but in others... it just became harder."

They were quiet for a few minutes before Michael reached out and grabbed Hannah's hand in both of his.

"No matter what anyone says or what anyone does, I will always be here and I will always make my way back to you if you ever feel like we're too far apart."

Hannah had tears in her eyes and she didn't know what to think. The only thing she could manage to get out was, "Why me?"

Michael smiled.

"Because you're everything I've asked God for in a wife, and Samuel is everything I ever wanted in a son."

"What about Abigail Miller? I thought she was interested in you." Hannah simply had to know. She didn't want there to be anymore confusion or dissension between her and the Miller's.

Michael simply shook his head. "She's okay as a person and very beautiful. But she's no Hannah King. You tend to doubt yourself, but you're more beautiful than ten Abigail Millers'. You have beautiful brown hair that reminds me of dark chocolate and rich brown eyes to match. You have cute freckles on your nose that almost seem to contract when you squint your eyes just right... and when you get embarrassed or upset, your face gets really red and it's actually kind of cute." He winked at her.

Despite the tears, she managed to laugh at the last part. She didn't know if she should be rejoicing for herself or praying for Abigail. She loved Abigail like a little sister and would rather have her happy. As if

Michael could suddenly read her mind, he pulled his hands away and gave an exasperated sigh.

"Hannah, Hannah. Why can't you just take the gift that God is giving you? Stop pushing His free love away and stop pushing me away. I'm not usually one to give ultimatums, but if you can't make up your mind, then maybe we shouldn't even try." With that, Michael stood up and went to the kitchen to finish washing the dishes. As he left the living room he called back, "When you're done in there, go ahead and let yourself out. Thank you for coming over."

It was at that moment that Hannah realized she had just potentially thrown her life away. She couldn't move from her spot as much as she didn't want to be there anymore, but she had to do something. So she got down on her knees and just began crying out to the Lord for all of the things she had done to push the people in her life away. She had never done this before, and it was weird to do it in a place that wasn't even familiar, but she knew she needed to do it and she didn't care who could see her.

She didn't know how long she was there for, but when she opened up her eyes and wiped the tears away, she noticed that both Samuel and Michael were on their faces as well, crying and praying along with her. Michael was closest to her, so she put her hand on his back. He began to shake and sob even louder.

When he finally quieted down, she put her mouth down by his ear and whispered, "All I want is you, Michael. I give myself to you."

He breathed a heavy sigh and finally forced himself up. They looked into each other's eyes and knew this was only the beginning of something much deeper than either of them could fathom. He smiled a crooked smile as Samuel sat up with tears still streaming down his face.

"Geez, if you wanted a revival meeting, why didn't you just set one up with the elders?"

Two days later was Sunday, and the town went to church as usual. Michael grabbed Hannah and Samuel on their way out and asked them to stay a few more minutes with him.

"I have something I want to say to the elders and I want you to be there when I do."

"Both of us?" Hannah asked curiously.

"Of course. You come as the whole package." He smiled at them and Samuel couldn't contain his excitement over the mysterious way Michael was acting.

As soon as the last of the churchgoers had left and there were only the elders and the trio, Michael made his move.

"Excuse me, I have something I would like to propose."

The elders looked at him curiously and the preacher said, "Go on."

"I would like for Hannah to be my assistant for the rest of the school year. I know you told her that she couldn't, but the rule that she would be partial to her son is a little silly, since I've seen her in action and she's only more strict on him. These last three weeks have been a huge transition into a position I've never really had before, and Hannah has made everything I've done seem like it was extremely easy."

"We will consider your request, but we can't make any promises," the preacher seemed to be the speaker of the elders today.

"There's also another thing that you might want to consider," Michael seemed to be struggling with this one a little more. He looked at Hannah for just a moment and she nodded, not knowing what he was going to say but showing her support in whatever was about to happen.

"I want to marry her too."

The elders went into a tizzy trying to wrap their heads around this proclamation.

"What? You want to marry a widow?"

"What about children of your own?"

"What about Abigail Miller? Surely she's the better fit."

All of these quick suggestions cut Hannah's heart like a knife, but Michael stopped them all with a wave of his hand.

"My mind's been made up. I love Hannah King and have since I watched her stand up to you almost four weeks ago. And I love Samuel. He's dedicated his life for God's use only and he's everything I always prayed I would have in a son. As for Abigail, God will give her the right man at the right time. I'm not that man, and this is not that time."

The elders simply couldn't believe what they were hearing, but suddenly decided they needed to act right then. They quickly shuffled out of the sanctuary into a back room to discuss, leaving Michael, Hannah, and Samuel alone.

Hannah started to feel those doubts come in again, but this time she stopped them before they could start. *I have a man for the first time in years that loves me like God loves me! How can I ever say no to that kind of love?*

Samuel was starting to get anxious, but Michael wouldn't let him leave, so they began playing a game of tag in the sanctuary. Hannah sat and watched them play, laughing at the way Michael looked, behaving like a 5-year-old.

After almost an hour, the elders finally emerged from the back room. Some of them looked overjoyed and others looked pensive. Hannah wasn't sure if that was a good sign, but she braced her heart for anything.

"Don't." Michael had come up behind her and must have seen her body language. "Don't close your heart. Open it up. Allow yourself to feel. How can you love if you don't let yourself get hurt once in awhile?"

Hannah wasn't sure how to answer that question, but she didn't have the time. Samuel abruptly stopped gallivanting and returned to his place by his mother's side.

The preacher spoke. "We have considered your requests and have but one condition." He looked at the three of them equally. "That you must stay in this town for the rest of your lives and give your lives to serving the children of this community. They need people with big hearts like yours, and this town needs people with new hope to bring a fresh perspective."

"Wait, I have to stay here for the rest of my life?" Samuel asked. "Can't I go home?"

They all laughed as Michael explained he had to stay in the town, not in the church itself. "Ooohhh. Cool!"

Hannah was in shock that they were actually letting this happen. "You're okay with us getting married?"

"God has ordained every man, a wife." The preacher submitted. "And God has ordained every woman, a husband. You have been blessed enough to have been ordained two husbands. The favor of God is on your life, child. We know you won't do anything that would hurt us with it."

Michael pulled her into a hug, as he was still in shock that they said yes. He began to cry into her hair as she cried into his chest. They were going to get to start fresh on everything. And it was the best feeling ever.

Abigail still came to the school everyday to see Michael. Maybe she was hoping she could change his mind, because by now the whole town knew that Michael and Hannah were courting to be married. By the end of that first week, Hannah finally pulled Abigail aside and asked her what was going on.

"I just can't believe that a handsome man like Michael would fall for a widow like you."

Hannah did all she could not to choke the woman out with a bunch of children still around. She wanted to be a good example.

"Well, my dear, I'm sorry that you didn't get your way this time. I guess when it comes to matters of the heart, you're just not the expert."

Abigail huffed, "Who made you the judge on what I'm expert in?"

"Well I know good wife material when I see it, honey. If you want I can help you hone that passion a little better so that people start to take you more seriously. Men like a woman that can really stand up for herself without looking like a 5-year-old."

Abigail looked as if she'd been accosted, but she gathered her composure enough to curtly say, "Maybe I would like that."

Hannah smiled, hoping for only the best in this situation. "Alright then. I'll see you tonight at my house."

"Tonight?"

"Yes. If you want a husband, we must start right away."

"No, I can't do tonight! I have plans."

"With?"

Abigail suddenly looked very flustered. "Someone."

Hannah's eyebrows shot up. "A boy?"

"It's none of your business!" And she picked up the dress from around her heels and marched down the hill.

"What was that all about?" Michael asked as Hannah came back in to finish getting the room ready for tomorrow.

"Abigail's been seeing someone, but she's been coming up here everyday for you. I was nice, but I basically told her she needed to stop."

"I never heard you use those words. It actually sounded as if you were genuinely interested in her life."

Hannah smiled. "It's not like I'm not. I still want to see her do well, even though in her eyes I stole the man she wanted."

Michael stopped what he was doing and pulled her into him. "Hey." He looked deep into her eyes until it felt like he was seeing into her soul.

"No one stole me from anyone. I am my own person and I make my own decisions. Take those thoughts out of your mind right now."

Hannah closed her eyes to clear her head. Suddenly she felt something on her lips. She opened her eyes and saw that Michael was kissing her! She instinctively pulled back and it shocked him.

"What's wrong?"

"Let's... do that again."

This time she was prepared. And it was a glorious kiss with so much emotion and passion behind it. Hannah wasn't sure what had happened last Friday when they were on the floor of his living room, but since then their relationship seemed to be on a fast-track. It was overwhelming at times, but in times like this it felt just right. This was the healing that she needed after Joab died.

As Michael pulled away from Hannah and they looked at each other again, she told him, "Just now was the first time I've thought of Joab in a longing way in a week. Should I feel bad about that?"

Michael shook his head. "The memories of those we loved will always be there, but we have to learn to move on. Thinking of Joab in a longing way meant that even while I was trying to make a move, you were shutting me out. And you did. Now that you've experienced some healing and given a lot of that hurt to God, there's room in your heart to love again."

He suddenly became very serious as he got down on one knee and pulled a small box out of his pocket. He opened it as he spoke to reveal a gold ring with a small diamond set in it.

"With this ring I want you to promise me that you will always be open and vulnerable to me about what's going on. That you will tell me when you're hurting and that you'll tell me when we can rejoice together."

She nodded, too overwhelmed to speak. Her vision became cloudy as he finished his speech.

"As I give you this ring, I promise that I will always protect you and lead you in the ways that God is showing me to take. I promise that I will love and care for Samuel as my own and that he will be my own son... just as you will be my own wife."

Hannah managed to squeak out a "yes" as she threw her arms around her beloved Michael and they cried.

"I love you, my crying widow." They both laughed through the tears as they knew this would certainly not be the last time they cried together.

Their foundation was built solidly on the passion of teaching children and leading each other into the deeper things of God. Hannah knew that this was the best way to start any marriage, and she was blessed to get a second chance to do it all again. This time, she knew it would be for eternity.

When Amish Love Finds A Way

Stephanie Swift

"Katherine, for the love of all things holy and good, will you please stop?"

Katherine Mills sat upright on the church pew and furrowed a brow at her younger brother, Jonah. The worship service would be starting soon, but she couldn't concentrate after discovering one of the buttons on Jonah's shirt was missing. She turned his wrist over to inspect the cuff...again.

"Why didn't you mention it this morning?" she whispered. "I could've mended it before we left."

Jonah jerked his arm from her grasp as his eyes roamed over the congregation. An elderly woman seated in front of them passed a snide glance their way, but the old gossipmonger was the least of her concern.

"Katherine, I'm not a kid anymore. It can wait. Now please stop embarrassing me."

Katherine laced her fingers together on top of her lap and turned her attention to Bishop Abram, who was slowly making his way to the podium at the front of the sanctuary. Her embarrassing Jonah? The thought nearly made her laugh out loud. Oh please...as if he didn't do an excellent job of that on his own. Katherine rolled her eyes heavenward when she caught him winking at a couple of single women sitting on the opposite side of the church.

"Really, Jonah, don't you have any manners?"

He chuckled at her remark before the Bishop garnered the congregation's attention. A hush fell over the crowd and they all bowed their heads when he started the service with a long prayer. She made a mental note to mend Jonah's shirt as soon as they returned home. Perhaps he didn't mind going out in public with tattered clothing, but it bothered her to no end. The last thing she wanted or needed was for the people in their little Amish village to think she was slacking in caring for her brother, a job she'd taken very seriously since their parents' death three years prior.

When Katherine opened her eyes, she was surprised to see someone had joined Bishop Abram behind the podium, but it was no ordinary person, and the stranger certainly wasn't from their community. The gentleman standing beside the Bishop was dressed in English clothing, sporting a short beard and mustache, and he held a cell phone in his right hand. Katherine felt her cheeks flush, and she tried not to stare, but he was quite handsome.

The congregation shared curious glances as the Bishop gestured to the man and introduced him as Dr. Steven Read, a newcomer to Lancaster, but no foreigner to the Amish. He explained how the doctor was raised in the faith as a child in western Pennsylvania, and that he'd discovered his calling in life during his Rumspringa when he was just sixteen years old. He'd practiced medicine ever since and had recently taken over Lancaster's small medical clinic after the previous owner retired from the field.

"My brothers and sisters, I hope you will join me in welcoming Dr. Read to Lancaster and to our community. Several of you have mentioned to me how time-consuming it is to make the trip to the clinic, and Dr. Read has generously volunteered to make house calls."

The excitement in the room was almost palpable and Katherine felt her stomach flutter with excitement also. She'd lost count of the numerous times she'd wrangled Jonah into their carriage and made the long drive to the clinic - sometimes in the dead of night and even during torrential downpours. As far as she knew, the previous doctor never made house calls, at least not to the Amish households, so this was a welcomed change for sure.

After the Bishop introduced Dr. Read and concluded his discussion over the services he would provide, Katherine expected the doctor to leave, but he didn't. Instead, he sat down on one of the front pews and joined in the service. A couple of hours later, when Bishop Abram asked if he'd like to close the service with a prayer, he didn't falter or try to beg his way out of it. He wholeheartedly accepted, and his prayer even received a rousing "amen" from the Bishop when he finished.

Katherine struggled in vain to keep from ogling him, but she couldn't help herself. There was something oddly fascinating about the man - and it wasn't just his rugged good looks either.

"Really, Katherine, don't you have any manners? Stop staring." Jonah mimicked as they stood to leave. Her cheeks burned a bright shade of red as she playfully elbowed him in the stomach, which made him laugh. Two of his close friends caught his attention as they waved to him from across the crowded room, and when he left her side to join them, she was grateful for the reprieve.

Bishop Abram and the doctor stood by the front door, and as Katherine watched him smile and introduce himself to each member of the congregation, she stole a glance toward the back door of the church. Unfortunately, the throng of people was too big to push through so a hasty retreat in the opposite direction wasn't possible.

"Dr. Read, this is Katherine Mills. She and her younger brother, Jonah, own and operate the local dairy farm."

Katherine jerked her head around, not realizing the fast-moving crowd had already nudged her to the front of the line. When she nearly bumped into the doctor, she took a couple of hesitant steps backward to regain her footing.

"H-hello. It's nice meeting you. Welcome to Lancaster," she stammered.

The doctor grinned and thanked her, and Katherine felt her heartrate escalate when the masculine aroma of his cologne wafted past her nose and left her temporarily dazed. He pulled a business card from his jacket pocket and handed it to her, and when their fingers touched, she held her breath.

"Please don't hesitate to call me anytime you have an emergency - day or night," he remarked.

She didn't trust herself to say anything else without sounding like an enamored schoolgirl, so she simply nodded before turning to leave. Perhaps it was just wishful thinking, but she could almost feel the doctors gaze on her as she walked away, which made her legs wobbly and sent a chill up her spine.

Katherine sighed.

She couldn't deny it. The new doctor in town had her spellbound.

* * * *

Steven squinted as he peered out his car window, trying to discern which of the small houses belonged to Miss Hannah Bowen. He glanced at his notepad again and mumbled the information he'd hastily scribbled down while rushing out the door of his clinic.

"House #142. Okay...where are you?"

It was his first medical call to the small Amish village since Bishop Abram introduced him to everyone the previous Sunday, and his stomach flip-flopped with equal parts excitement and fear. He wanted to make a good impression, but as he circled back for what felt like the hundredth time, he started to wonder if he may have bitten off more than he could chew. With the sun setting on the horizon, most of the houses looked identical in the fading light, from their brown tin roofs straight down to the white wooden swings on their front porches.

He strongly considered throwing in the towel until he caught sight of an older woman standing on some porch steps, waving her arms high in the air to get his attention. As he brought his car to a stop in front of the house, he caught sight of the small metallic numbers nailed to one of the porch columns - #142. When he turned off the ignition and stepped out with his medical bag in tow, the woman left the steps and walked around the vehicle to greet him.

"Miss Bowen?" he inquired.

She nodded and motioned toward the front door. "*Yah*, thank you so much for coming, Dr. Read. My son, William, woke up this morning with a fever, and he's been sleeping off and on all day, which isn't like him because he's usually full of energy."

He could tell by the way her voice shook that she was worried, and as they made their way inside the small wood framed house he understood why. A young man who couldn't have been more than twelve years old stood just inside the doorway, holding on to the back of a tall chair. His unruly brown hair was plastered to his skin and his face was a deathly shade of white.

"William!" Miss Bowen exclaimed. "What are you doing up?"

He opened his mouth but no words came out, which alarmed Steven right away. He noticed how William swayed precariously on his feet, and he rushed over to keep him upright before he toppled to the floor.

"Your mom is right. We should get you back to bed."

When he put his arm around William's waist to keep him steady, his heart plummeted to his feet when he felt the intense heat emanating from William's body through his clothing.

"Miss Bowen, can you please bring me some ice wrapped in a bath cloth or dish towel? He's burning up with fever and we need to get it down as quickly as we can."

Tears cascaded down her face as she directed him to William's room before racing to the kitchen. Once William was lying comfortably on his bed, Steven opened his medical bag and removed a stethoscope and otoscope so he could listen to his chest and examine his ears and throat. Fortunately, his lungs sounded clear, but his ears and throat were extremely red and inflamed, which could explain the fever.

Miss Bowen returned with the ice and placed the towel against William's forehead. He opened his eyelids slightly and moaned, and Miss Bowen kissed his cheeks and caressed them gently with her fingers.

"It's okay, sweetheart. I know you're hurting, but Dr. Read is going to help you feel better. I promise."

He appreciated her show of confidence in him, especially since he was basically a stranger to her small town, and he smiled before continuing his examination. The lymph nodes in William's neck were swollen and tender, and although the ice brought his fever down somewhat, it still wasn't where Steven felt it needed to be.

"Miss Bowen, William's ears and throat are badly infected, and I would like to give him a shot of Rocephin, if it's alright with you. This medicine will take care of his fever more quickly than taking oral medication, and I'm worried if we don't get his fever down soon he might have a seizure."

As soon as Steven mentioned giving him a shot, William's eyelids flew open and he fervently shook his head while Miss Bowen struggled to keep him still. "No, no, no...I don't want a shot..." he mumbled.

Steven reached out and touched her hand. "Miss Bowen, I know how you feel about traditional medicine, and I understand because I was raised in an Amish household, but I promise I wouldn't recommend this if I didn't feel it was absolutely necessary."

The tears kept rolling down her cheeks, and the inner battle going on inside was more than evident by the pained look on her face. He felt guilty for suggesting something he knew was against her faith, but he had to do what he felt was right for William. Whether she decided to do it or not was totally up to her, but he feared there would be dire consequences if she refused. William's eyes swelled with tears, which only added to his misery, and he swallowed hard to try and keep it together. He dearly loved his job, but there were moments when he wished he'd never left home, and this was one of those times.

"Luke! Come here please!" Miss Bowen called.

Steven heard a door open in the hallway moments before a youngster appeared in the doorway. This child looked younger than

William by a couple of years, but they were almost identical with their wavy brown hair and blue eyes.

"What's wrong with brother?" he asked. His eyes were wide and expressive as he gazed at William, and Steven felt helpless and unsure of what to say. He'd tended to many children in his line of work, but having none of his own left him at a disadvantage sometimes.

"He's sick, and I need you to get Mr. Jonah right away. Do you understand?"

Without another word, Luke turned and bolted down the hallway and out the front door.

"Jonah Mills has been like a second father to my boys since my husband passed away last year," she explained. "Maybe he can help keep William calm while you give him the shot."

Steven thought for a moment. *Jonah Mills.* The name sounded vaguely familiar, and his spirits lifted when he remembered Bishop Abram introducing Jonah as Katherine's younger brother. He'd met dozens of people that Sunday in church, but Katherine was the only person he hadn't been able to stop thinking about, especially after Bishop Abram made it a point to mention to him that she wasn't married.

A few minutes later, Steven heard the front door open and he held his breath anxiously as heavy footsteps echoed down the hallway before Luke reappeared with Jonah by his side. They were both out of breath and Jonah's face paled when he saw William lying motionless on the bed. Steven leaned over and looked behind them, hoping that Katherine may have followed, but his hopes vanished when he realized it was just the two of them.

Jonah knelt by the bed and William's eyelids fluttered open when he heard him speak. "Hey, buddy. I got here as fast as I could."

Miss Bowen reciprocated the dishcloth between different spots on William's body, from his forehead to his cheeks and downward to his chest. "Dr. Read was just telling us how it would make William feel better if he gave him a shot to bring down his fever, but he doesn't like that idea very much."

Jonah nodded as if he understood before grabbing William's right hand and giving it a squeeze. "Our baseball game won't be the same next weekend if we don't have our best hitter there to help lead us to victory. I bet Dr. Read is great at giving shots. You probably won't even feel it."

He gave Steven a stern look, as if needing reassurance, so Steven reiterated to William that he would do his very best to make the shot as pain-free as possible. A couple of tears escaped and rolled down William's cheeks, but he ultimately agreed to it, and while Jonah, Luke, and Miss Bowen showered him with words of encouragement, Steven removed the bottle of Rocephin and a syringe from his medical bag and prepared the dosage.

Although it seemed to last an eternity, the amount of time it took between turning William over on his left side and Steven giving him the shot in his hip was mere seconds, and he was pleasantly surprised when William smiled at him when it was over.

"See? That wasn't so bad," Jonah said. "I'm really proud of you, buddy. You'll start feeling better in no time."

After Steven returned his supplies to his bag, he gestured for Miss Bowen to follow him into the hallway. While Luke took over holding the dishcloth to William's forehead, Jonah regaled him with jokes that had him laughing and smiling. When Steven saw the color return to William's cheeks, he breathed a huge sigh of relief.

"I'll come by tomorrow afternoon and check on him," Steven whispered, so they wouldn't be overheard. "Hopefully he'll be feeling a lot better and he won't have to take antibiotics, but we'll just play it by ear and see how he's doing."

Before Miss Bowen could reply, there was a knock on the front door, and Steven's heart skipped a beat when she opened it and he saw Katherine standing on the other side. Her long brown hair was pulled back and tied with a white ribbon at the base of her neck, and her cheeks were flushed a bright shade of pink.

"Is something wrong?" she asked, while trying to catch her breath. "I would have been here sooner, but I was getting dinner out of the oven when Luke came by, and all I heard was "William needs you" before he and Jonah took off running. I had no idea what was going on and I ran the whole way and..."

Miss Bowen raised a hand to stop her from staying anything else, which was probably a good thing, because she appeared on the verge of hyperventilating. When Miss Bowen ushered her inside and she caught sight of Steven standing in the living room, she flashed him a bashful smile. "Hello, Dr. Read. How are you?"

Steven felt tongue-tied at first, but he forced himself to say something – *anything*. "I'm doing good. Please...call me Steven."

Miss Bowen excused herself and returned to William's room, and suddenly the room became eerily quiet and very awkward. Katherine crossed her arms over her chest and rocked back and forth on her heels while Steven stuffed his hands inside his pants pockets and tried to come up with some topic of conversation.

Why was it so difficult talking to her? It wasn't as if he hadn't talked to other women before. It was ridiculous, really, and he felt embarrassed over his lack of wisdom when it came to the opposite sex.

"How is William doing?" she asked.

Steven cleared his throat before trusting himself to say anything coherent without tripping over his own tongue. "His throat and ears are badly infected, but I believe he's going to be okay. At first, he was afraid of getting a shot, but Jonah was able to talk him into it."

His comment made her smile, and Steven's heart fluttered. She was so beautiful, and her happiness lit up the entire room. He couldn't help but wonder if she even realized just how beautiful she was.

"Jonah is a lot older than William, but they are really close."

Katherine walked over to a chair in the living room and sat down, so Steven followed suit and took a seat on the sofa across from her. He could hear the muffled whispers streaming in the hallway, and his spirits lifted when he heard laughter coming from William's bedroom.

"Miss Bowen said he's become somewhat of a father figure since her husband died," he replied.

Katherine sat upright in her seat and flattened her palms on top of her knees. She looked uncomfortable, and he hoped it wasn't his presence that bothered her. If anything, he felt more at peace talking to her than he had since his arrival in Lancaster two months prior.

"*Yah*, I think it's good for them both. Our parents passed away three years ago, and there's only so much a sister knows about hunting, fishing, and farming. I do my fair share of it, but he needs more male friends in his life to talk to and spend time with."

Steven couldn't help but envy their closeness. When he didn't return home following his Rumspringa, he ruined any possibility of seeing or talking to his parents and two older brothers ever again. He didn't regret his decision to follow his dream of becoming a doctor, but he couldn't deny there were times when he wished he could go back and do things differently just to hear their voices one more time.

The sound of footsteps on the hardwood floor interrupted their conversation a few seconds before Jonah and Miss Bowen entered the living room.

"William is sleeping," she announced. "Thank you for coming so quickly, Dr. Read. He already seems to be feeling much better."

Steven took that as his cue to leave, even though it was the last thing he wanted to do. He would've been content just to sit and talk to Katherine all night. When he stood to go, she did the same, nearly causing them to bump into each other. They were so close he could see the tiny line of freckles that danced across the bridge of her nose.

"I should be going," he said. "I need to stop by the diner before they close."

Jonah waved a hand in the air, as if dismissing his comment. "Isabelle's Diner in Lancaster? No way. You can come to our house for a proper dinner. Katherine made her famous meatloaf and mashed potatoes."

He looked at Katherine, and he could tell by the bewildered expression on her face that she was shocked by her brother's suggestion. Because of that, he thought it would be best to politely decline, but before he had the opportunity, Katherine was agreeing with him. "I think that's a great idea."

He couldn't tell if she truly meant it or not, but he didn't want to be rude and ruin any chance he might have of seeing her again.

"Umm...okay," he replied, hesitantly. "Miss Bowen, I'll see you tomorrow afternoon, but if you need me before then, please don't hesitate to call me again."

She nodded before wishing them a good evening and leading them to the door. As Steven crossed the porch with Jonah and Katherine, he couldn't help but wonder what other surprises the rest of the night would hold.

* * * *

The following afternoon, while Jonah was busy gathering milk in the barn, Katherine took her cup of coffee to the back porch so she could enjoy a few minutes of peace and quiet. She also needed the coffee to keep her awake, since she'd gotten little sleep the night before. Although dinner ended early, she and Steven talked until midnight, and the remaining hours until daybreak were spent tossing and turning when she was unable to get him off her mind.

Katherine sighed contentedly as she recalled how easy it was to talk to him and the way his laughter reverberated off the walls in her tiny kitchen and wrapped around her heart. But despite the good that warmed her soul, there was also the hard truth that he'd been shunned from his own community when he didn't return from his Rumspringa.

He was now an English man who lived by English customs, and that was something she couldn't easily ignore, no matter how wildly her heart raced whenever he was near.

"What is causing such deep concentration, sister?"

Startled from her daydream, Katherine jumped and nearly spilled her full cup of coffee as Jonah laughed and bounded up the back-porch steps. When he sat down in the rocking chair beside her, she gave him a sideways glance without trying to hide her annoyance.

"I bet you were thinking about the new doctor in town," he joked. "Am I right?"

She didn't reply, but the blush in her cheeks must have given her away, as Jonah slapped his hand on the arm of the rocker and howled with laughter. "I knew it!"

Katherine steadied her cup of coffee on her lap and looked out across the large field behind their house. Rain clouds hovered in the distance and cast a shadow over the yard, but she didn't mind the impending rain. In fact, she welcomed it. If anything, it matched her solemn mood.

"I guess you think you're pretty clever, the way you snuck past me and invited him to eat dinner with us last night."

Jonah laughed again. "Oh, come on. You know you enjoyed it. I could hear the two of you talking and laughing from my bedroom."

Katherine sighed once again. "You're forgetting the circumstances, Jonah. Even if I wanted to be with Steven, it wouldn't be possible. He's already been shunned from our way of life, so no one would accept him."

Jonah frowned. "I don't think that's true. I know he and Bishop Abram are good friends, so there might be more hope than you realize."

Katherine took a sip of her coffee and let the heat from it sink into her bones. There was a lot to consider, but she was honestly afraid to get her hopes up and risk them being trampled on. There were also more important things to keep in mind besides her own feelings over the matter.

"I'm not going to leave you, Jonah. I made a promise to myself when mom and dad died that I would watch over you and take care of you – always."

From the corner of her eye, she caught Jonah turning in the rocker so he could face her, but she refused to look at him. She knew what would be behind those brown eyes, and she didn't want to see it. She'd lost count of the times they'd discussed their future and she didn't want to hear him proclaim again how he would be fine on his own someday. Perhaps he would when he found the right woman to settle down with, but until then he was her responsibility.

"Katherine, I love you, but you have *got* to accept the fact that I'm eighteen years old and a grown man."

Katherine cocked a weary eyebrow as she glanced in his direction. "I'm fully aware of that, Jonah."

He took off his hat and propped it on top of his knee. "There's no way I could ever properly thank you for everything you've done for me, but I want you to be happy. That's all I've ever wanted."

Katherine took another sip of her coffee. "But I am happy."

Jonah reached out and laid a hand on her arm, causing her to stop rocking and look his way. He had the sincerest expression on his face – something she wasn't used to seeing, since he spent most of his time cracking jokes and doing his best to make her laugh.

"I'm talking about the happiness I saw last night, Katherine. I didn't miss the way your eyes lit up when Steven was here, and I don't want you to risk losing that over me. Father taught me everything I need to know about running his business, and I can take care of myself and this farm."

Katherine let her eyes sweep over the property before she shook her head. "There's no way you can handle this all on your own."

Jonah's lips curled upward into a sly grin. "Who said I would be alone? I do plan on getting married someday, and I even have my heart set on someone special right now. I have for quite a while now."

Katherine sat up straight in her seat, nearly spilling her coffee again. "Really? Who is she?"

Jonah rested his head against the back of the rocking chair and grinned. "Don't even try and change the subject. We're talking about *you* – not me. You'll find out soon enough."

Katherine couldn't help but wonder who he was referring to, as she carefully considered every single woman in their community. There were several who came to mind, but she knew he wouldn't divulge his secret no matter how hard she pushed, so she decided to let it pass – at least for the time being.

"So, what do you think I should do?" she asked. "Should I talk to Bishop Abram first to see where he stands with us seeing each other?"

Jonah looked up at the tin roof and shook his head. "I think you should follow your heart. What do you *want* to do first?"

Katherine smiled. That was an easy question. "I want to talk to Steven and see if he feels the same way about me."

Jonah grabbed his hat and jumped to his feet. "That's what I was hoping you'd say. You should do that...*now*."

Katherine nearly choked on her coffee. "What? I didn't mean right this second."

Unfortunately, he wouldn't be swayed. Jonah took the coffee cup from her hand and disappeared inside the house. When he returned a couple of minutes later, the cup was nowhere to be seen and he had an umbrella hooked over his forearm.

"Take this in case it starts raining on your way to the phone."

He pulled Steven's business card from his shirt pocket and handed it to her, along with the umbrella. Katherine looked toward the dark clouds in the west and frowned. What if she didn't make it back before it started pouring rain? The phone shanty was a mile or so from their home, and the storm clouds were approaching fast.

Katherine stood up straight and squared her shoulders. No, it was now or never. If she kept waiting she would lose her nerve...and she would never hear the end of it from Jonah. Katherine opened the back door and grabbed her rubber boots, which were nestled in a corner just inside the doorway, and slipped them on before she changed her mind.

"Wish me luck!" she called to her brother, as she bounded off the back-porch steps and walked hurriedly toward the main dirt road. Her heart pounded furiously inside her chest, but it was a wonderful feeling – a mixture of excitement, anxiousness, and hope all rolled into one.

She prayed out loud as she walked, which bolstered her confidence. She refused to believe that God would bring Steven into her life only to break her heart by keeping them apart. With any luck, Bishop Abram and the others would be on their side as well.

* * * *

Steven unlocked his front door and retreated inside his house. He'd managed to get his groceries from the store to the car before the rain started, but now he had to carry them from the car to his house before the paper bags turned to mush and his groceries spilled all over the driveway. He groaned as the fumbled for the light switch. He didn't even own an umbrella.

Steven pulled his cell phone from his jacket pocket and plugged it into his charger on the kitchen counter. He'd noticed the voicemail icon blinking while driving home, but there wasn't enough battery life remaining to check it. He did see on the caller ID that it was the number to the Amish village, which was strange. He'd visited William Bowen around noon, and he was doing much better, so it couldn't be his mother calling.

At least, he hoped it wasn't. Steven's heart sank when he considered the possibility William may have relapsed. He quickly got the groceries inside as he waited for the battery to charge, and when he finished putting the items away, he saw a green light blinking on his phone, signaling that the battery was charged enough for him to check his messages. When he heard the voice on the other end of the line, he was taken by surprise.

"Hello, Steven. I...I've never left a message before, so I don't know if I'm doing this right or not. First off, I'm okay and there isn't an emergency. I apologize if I'm being too forward by calling you, but...I just wanted to let you know how much I enjoyed our conversation last night..."

His heart skipped a beat. *Katherine.* There was a long pause, but he could hear a loud noise in the background that sounded like thunder, and Steven frowned when he pictured her in the village's small phone shanty while the rain poured outside.

"I know our lives are very different, but...that hasn't stopped me from thinking about you. I really don't know what else to say other than I hope to see you again...soon."

Click.

Steven glanced at his wristwatch as he gathered up his cell phone and car keys. Going by the timestamp on his caller ID, fifteen minutes had passed since Katherine's call. As he raced to his vehicle, he silently prayed that the emotion he heard in her voice was the same as he'd felt since the day he met her. She was right about their paths in life being completely different, but he hoped that wouldn't stand in the way of something he felt in his heart could be very special. He'd grown up with the same Amish values and traditions, so there was no denying it could possibly be an uphill battle.

Steven roared the car to life and took off toward Katherine's house. The rain had died down to a drizzle, but the dirt road leading to the village was slippery and sent his wheels spinning. He took his foot off the accelerator and tapped his fingers impatiently against the steering wheel. He wanted to get to her as quickly as he could, but he also needed to get there in one piece.

As he neared Katherine's driveway, he caught sight of her walking across the front yard to her house. When his headlights shined upon her, he noticed how the small umbrella she carried did nothing more than protect her face from the rain. The rest of her was soaking wet.

Steven parked the car and took off on foot to meet her. She stopped when she saw him coming, and when he put his arm around her waist and led her toward the front porch, she didn't object. Just as he guessed, she was soaked to the skin and she shivered so much her teeth chattered. He opened the door and ushered her inside, and while Jonah went to the kitchen to get her something warm to drink, Steven grabbed a blanket from the sofa and draped it around her shoulders.

"What in the world were you thinking, Katherine?" he murmured. "You're going to catch your death of cold..."

She stopped him mid-sentence by placing a hand against his chest. "If you got my message then it was worth it."

Steven ran his fingers through her wet hair and moved it away from her neck, letting his fingertips glide softly against her neck. "I did."

Jonah returned with a steaming cup of coffee, but the moment he saw them huddled close together, he placed the cup on a table beside the sofa and excused himself from the room – but not before winking and grinning at them both.

Steven pulled the blanket tighter around Katherine's shoulders. "You should change clothes before you get sick...doctor's orders."

She laughed softly and the beautiful sound melted his heart and weakened his knees. When she took his hand, and led him toward the sofa, he followed like a love-struck teenager. Once they were seated, he picked up the coffee mug and encouraged her take a couple of sips. The color returned to her cheeks, although a bit slowly for his liking, and his first concern was getting some heat coursing through her veins.

"Steven...am I crazy for thinking this could turn into something more than just friendship?" she asked.

He squeezed her hands and moved closer. "No, I don't think that's crazy at all. I know we haven't known each other long, but I feel the same way. Do you remember me telling you last night how I wished I could go back and do things differently – how I never would have left my family?"

She nodded.

"I feel very strongly about that, and I know the odds may be stacked against me, but I really feel like Bishop Abram and the community will give me the opportunity to return to the fold when they see how I feel about you. All we do is pray over it and hope for the best."

When Katherine leaned into him and gently kissed his lips, he was caught off guard, but happily so. The moment may have been brief, but it left his heart racing wildly in his chest.

"We'll get through this together," she replied, emphatically.

Steven nodded – more certain in his conviction than ever before. He knew deep in his heart they were meant to be together...and he was ready and willing to do whatever it took to make that dream a reality.

Amish Decisions

Samantha Collier

Rachel looked out the window, watching the fierce blizzard swirl around the farmhouse. It had been building for days.

Last night, it had intensified so much that her sleep was disturbed. The old house creaked and moaned as the wind picked up. She had risen to her bedroom window, amazed at the snowflakes swirling as if in a vortex. The cold had punctured her skin like a million needles.

This morning, it was worse. She watched, anxiously, as her father battled alone through it, securing the animals as best as he could.

Two day until Christmas. The world was white, and frightening. Somehow, nature reflected her inner turmoil. She had not been herself, these past weeks.

Sighing, Rachel wrapped her shawl tighter around her shoulders. The temperature had dropped, again. The fire roaring in the corner seemed to throw out little warmth. At least they had enough firewood to outlast the storm. How long could the blizzard last? Would Christmas still go ahead?

Suddenly, she heard her father shouting outside. What was wrong? She craned her neck to see, but the swirl of white was so intense outside that it was impossible.

The front door opened, sending in a blast of snow. It was her father, of course. But as Rachel turned, she was shocked to see two figures with him. Both tall. One was dressed in black, in the typical Amish fashion. The other wore jeans and a huge snow coat, in the English style. Two men, covered in snow, stomping their boots onto the mat.

Her father struggled to shut the door against the wind. Then the trio walked into the living room.

Rachel gasped. How could this be? For she knew the two men. They were as different from each other as chalk and cheese. As far as she knew, they didn't know each other. How was it that they were together, in her living room?

And worse, stuck together in her living room. For this blizzard was here to stay, at least for today. There was little indication that it would abate. The two men were marooned with her family at their farmhouse. The neighbours were miles away in either direction. And the roads would be blocked.

It was as if they had planned it, but how could they have?

Two men. Both known to Rachel. Had God planned it? He knew the decision that she had to make. Had he put both here to make her decide?

***

The Amish man was Abraham. She had known him forever.

She remembered the first time that she had seen him. They had been children, going to school together. Someone had pulled her *kapps* from behind as she sat at her desk, making her cry. Well, she had only been five years old. But the boy that she had been told to sit next to reached over and gave her his handkerchief. Through her sobs, she had turned and looked at him.

"Are you alright?" he whispered, looking at her in concern.

She nodded, slowly. Her sobs abated.

"I'm Abraham," he said. "Don't worry, I'll look out for you."

And he had. Abraham had been like the brother she had never had. In the playground, he would watch her, making sure she was okay. They rarely played together, but she knew he was always there. Like a guardian angel.

They had grown up, as children must. She was always conscious of him in her life. His eyes would shine when he looked at her. A constant, like the moon and the stars in the night sky.

Rachel could pinpoint the moment when it had all changed between them.

Rummspringa had happened. Rachel had been curious about the world, and travelled to stay with English friends in the city. She had seen so many wonderful things; the English world intoxicated her.

Should she stay in her community, safe and loved, or should she spread her wings wider? What did God intend for her life?

She had met him in town, when she had returned. Literally ran into him as she crossed the road to do her shopping.

"Abraham!" She had been joyful, to see him again. But he hadn't smiled back.

"Rachel." He inclined his head, quietly assessing her. "I haven't seen you for a while. Where have you been?"

"Oh, Abraham," she gushed. Her eyes shone in excitement. "I have been to the city! It was wonderful. So many things to see and do."

He had frowned, slightly. "*Jah,* it can be exciting," he had replied. He looked her over. "You've changed, Rachel."

"Have I?" She twirled around, inviting his admiration. But it wasn't forthcoming. His statement hadn't been a compliment. She felt her excitement puncture slowly. Why was he so disapproving?

"Well, it was nice to see you," she replied. She didn't smile at him. "I must go, now. Mamm is waiting for me."

He had bowed again, and walked away without a backward glance.

And that was it. She hadn't talked to him much since. A distance that could not be bridged had sprung up between them. She heard that he was courting Eva, a girl they had both gone to school with. She had been sad that they hadn't remained friends, but philosophical, too. For her world had changed entirely.

David, the English man in her living room, had happened.

She had met him on *rummspringa.* He was a friend of the family she had stayed with. She had been shy with him, at first. She hadn't met many English men. But he had been gentle and sweet with her, asking how she was enjoying the city. Then he had invited her to see the latest exhibition of an artist that was showing at a gallery.

She had hesitated, just for a moment. But then she had accepted.

He picked her up in his car, whirling through the city streets. She wasn't used to cars, and felt quite giddy.

They had walked through the gallery together, admiring the paintings. She didn't know much about art, but David was well informed. He pointed out how the artist had used texture and shading to build the paintings. He knew a lot about the history of art, and the influences in the paintings.

She hadn't said much. It was like she was a sponge, soaking in all the knowledge that was being heaped upon her. It was fascinating, and alluring.

Could she become a part of this world?

But then, *rummspringa* had ended, and she had returned home. Her afternoon at the gallery with David acquired the aura of a pleasant dream. She knew it had happened, and that it had been wonderful. But she had not seen him again.

Until he had unexpectedly visited her.

Mamm had been shocked when she opened the door on the tall English man that day.

"*Jah*?" she had inquired, looking him up and down. "Can I help you?"

David had smiled. "Yes, I was wondering if Rachel was here," he said.

Rachel had heard his voice and come to the door, amazed. "It's alright, Mamm," she said. "This is David, a friend of the Baileys. I met him on my stay there."

Mamm had raised her eyebrows, but let him enter.

David had walked into the house, a bit awkwardly. She had made them coffee; her mother had left them to talk alone in the parlour. Rachel was mystified. Why was he here?

It turned out that David had friends in the area, and knew she was close by.

"I was wondering," he said, looking at her carefully, "whether you would like to see the gallery in the nearest town. And then maybe, get a coffee?"

Rachel had considered. She was very fond of David, but he was an Englisher. Would going on outings with him encourage him to think that she might court him?

She didn't even know, herself. It was like she was being pulled in two directions. One path, very clear and obvious – getting baptised into her community, and living the life her family wanted her to. The other path was thorny, and wound into complicated areas – to not be baptised, and so become a part of the English world. Her father had started pressuring her recently about it, to make the choice. He also wanted her to consider marriage.

I'm only nineteen, Rachel thought to herself, a bit desperately. Why must I make a choice?

But she did. If only she could be like her best friend, Lovina, who was very sure and comfortable about staying within the community. But then, Lovina had courted several local Amish boys, and knew how to talk to them. Lovina wasn't shy and nervy, like Rachel.

Rachel took a sip of her coffee, thinking deeply. David needed an answer. He had sought her out, and besides, it would be impolite to refuse him. And she did like him, very much.

"I would love to," she replied. David smiled.

She very much felt like she was on the edge of a precipice, where one wrong step could see her careering into an abyss.

***

Rachel looked at the two men, frozen from the blizzard. She could feel her mouth open, like a gaping fish. Surprise had rendered her speechless.

Abraham spoke first. "You look surprised, Rachel," he said. "I was travelling along the road when I saw a car broken down."

"Yes," David continued, looking at Abraham, "my car suddenly broke down. The electrics I think; the lights were dimming and the radio flickering on and off. Luckily, Abraham happened by and gave me a lift in his buggy."

"But the blizzard caught us, and your farmhouse was closest," Abraham continued. "So here we are."

Both men looked at her, expectantly.

Rachel roused herself. "Please, sit down," she said. At least her powers of speech had returned. "I will make a pot of coffee, and inform my mother. She is sewing in her room."

Abraham and David sat down, looking at each other warily. You could cut the air with a knife, Rachel thought darkly.

They would all just have to make the best of it. At least until the blizzard cleared.

***

As Rachel made the coffee, she thought back to the week before, when she had gone into town with David to the gallery.

It had started out perfectly fine. They had perused the gallery, and Rachel had enjoyed it again. She was getting a stronger sense of art in the English world; was becoming infected with David's passion for it. Once again, the world seemed to shift and slide for her. She could – if she made the choice – do this all the time.

But what of her family? They would be devastated if she decided not to be baptised. Oh, it wasn't the same as if she left them after being baptised, she knew that. She wouldn't be shunned. But she would still be forever separate from them. She would be able to see them, but she knew it would never be the same.

Yet, the siren's call of the gallery beckoned her. A life, perhaps, with this man? Where they could talk about art, view it, travel together?

She was getting ahead of herself, of course. She didn't know how she felt about David.

It seemed she didn't know anything, anymore. The confusion, the push and pull of it, was like a fog within her brain.

They had a coffee afterwards, where David had spoken enthusiastically about the exhibition, and the artist.

"Would you like to come with me to another?" he asked, his eyes shining. "There is one in the next town starting next week."

"Maybe," Rachel had replied, frowning. "I'm not sure."

"Didn't you enjoy today?" he asked quickly. He seemed to really want to hear the answer.

"*Jah*, it was wonderful," she said. She paused, trying to gather her thoughts. "It's just that I am confused. I don't know if it is the best idea, doing this too much. It lures me away from my community."

He nodded, seeming to understand. "But then you can make an informed decision, can't you?" he pressed. "The more knowledge you have, the more power."

"Maybe," she replied, sipping her coffee. "Or maybe it is more temptation." She smiled, then shook her head. "I will let you know, David."

The shop bell rang, and someone walked through the door. She turned to look.

It was Abraham.

Would he acknowledge her? He barely spoke to her, anymore. It was sad; she remembered when they had been friends. Must everything change?

He had seen her. He paused, as if considering if he should approach.

Her heart lifted when he turned in her direction, heading toward the table.

"Rachel." He nodded at them both, his eyes widening slightly as he assessed David. Was he terribly shocked to see her here, having coffee with an Englisher? Would he disapprove?

"Abraham," she said, smiling widely. "It is so good to see you! This is my friend, David."

The men shook hands. Rachel could see David was quietly assessing Abraham, as well.

"So," Abraham said. He shifted awkwardly. "Have you been busy?"

"We've just been to see the latest exhibition at the gallery," Rachel replied. "Oh, you would love it, Abraham! Such beautiful paintings."

Abraham nodded, slowly. "I am glad you enjoyed it," he said. "Well, I must be off." He tilted his hat, at them both. Then he turned to the counter, to order what he had come in for.

"An old friend of yours?" asked David.

"One of my oldest," answered Rachel, a little sadly. "But we have drifted apart, lately. He doesn't want to be friends with me anymore, it seems." She looked down at her coffee, biting her lip.

"Well, he doesn't deserve you, then," said David, reaching out to put his hand over hers.

She stared down at his hand, covering her own. Was it seemly, especially in public? But she didn't move it.

And it was at that moment that Abraham turned back to them.

He frowned, looking at their hands. She could feel tension zip through his body, making him stand straighter. Almost as if he were about to pounce.

She quickly removed her hand, blushing. What must Abraham think of her?

The moment seemed to stretch on, forever. David locked eyes with Abraham, who stared him down. Tension filled the air.

Eventually, Abraham had broken it. He had simply turned and walked out of the shop, not looking back.

Rachel's eyes filled with tears. She couldn't bear him thinking badly of her. But what could she do now?

***

And now they were both sitting in her parlour, awaiting coffee. Life was strange, Rachel reflected as she picked up the cups and took them into the waiting men.

Her father had re-joined them, and was in the process of throwing a log onto the fire. It hissed and crackled as it fell, shooting out sparks up into the chimney. Inside, all was warm and bright; outside, the world had turned to white, a swirling vortex of snowflakes. The old house creaked and groaned under the pressure.

Rachel looked at the candles adorning the windows. The Christmas baskets, that had been prepared for the elderly in the community by her mother, were sitting on the floor, awaiting delivery. Would they be able to deliver them, now? It was only two days until Christmas. Rachel's heart constricted at the thought that those baskets would not get to their recipients in time.

Abraham was still sitting, staring at the fire and chatting with her father. David had stood up, and was looking out the window. He was frowning.

"It doesn't look like I'll be making it home for Christmas," he said, a little sadly. Rachel walked up to him, smiling.

"It might clear," she said, staring out. "I have seen blizzards suddenly blow themselves out. You might still make it." She pondered the thought of spending Christmas away from her family. She simply couldn't imagine it. She pictured them all gathered, eating a huge roast chicken with gravy and all the trimmings, just like they always did. Afterwards, there would be pie.

Christmas was about family. She shuddered. If she decided not to get baptised, she would no longer be a part of it. She couldn't bear the thought.

She could feel Abraham's eyes on her. Was he disapproving of her, again? Why had he suddenly decided that he didn't like her anymore? It was so perplexing. To have been so close to him, for so long.

They made stilted conversation as the day wore into the night. Her mother made up the spare bedrooms, and eventually they had all retired for the night. Rachel breathed a sigh of relief; she was glad to have escaped.

In bed, she pondered further. Eventually she turned to her bible, seeking comfort. A verse from Proverbs leapt out at her: "Trust in the Lord with all your heart, and do not lean on your own understanding. In all your ways acknowledge him, and he will make straight your paths."

She reflected. Perhaps there was her answer. She had been trying so hard to solve the dilemma, on an intellectual level. Perhaps she needed to stop thinking, and start trusting God. If she calmed her mind enough, he would lead her where she was supposed to go. She needed to stop fighting so hard.

She sighed, frowning. In the confusion of the two men staying unexpectedly, she had forgotten to get herself a glass of water before bed, as was her habit. She got up, sliding on her slippers and dressing gown, padding quietly down the stairs.

She had just turned on the tap and was filling the glass when she heard a sound behind her. She turned. David was standing there, looking at her.

Rachel instinctively tightened the belt on her dressing gown. This wasn't good; she was in her night attire, and didn't have her prayer *kapps* on. He shouldn't see her like this. She took the glass, smiling slightly at him as she walked past him.

He grabbed her arm, making her turn around to face him.

"David," she said, under her breath. "What are you doing? You are hurting me."

In response, he gripped her arm tighter, pulling her against him. The glass wobbled precariously in her hand. She didn't like the way that he was looking at her, not at all. What had suddenly come over him?

"Rachel, I want to kiss you," he said. Her eyes widened, in horror.

"No," she whispered. "It's not proper. This is my home, and you must respect our rules. I don't know how I feel about you, David. I know I like you as a friend."

He let go of her arm, suddenly, so that she stumbled backwards. Water spilt from the glass, slopping onto the floor.

"I should have known," he hissed at her. "You've been leading me on, all this time. Don't act innocent."

"I have not!" she replied. The accusation stung her. "You wanted to spend time with me, as a friend. That's what we've been doing. I never led you to believe anything else!"

He looked at her, witheringly. Then he turned and walked out of the room.

She leaned against the kitchen bench, breathing heavily.

What had just happened? She couldn't believe it. This was David, who had been nothing but kind and tender with her. Where had this sudden anger toward her come from? What had she done wrong?

Her eyes filled with tears of confusion and hurt. She had wanted to be part of the English world, had been dipping her toes into it. It had seemed expansive, full of things she wanted to explore. But this...this was a side of it, that she didn't like at all.

Was there truth in David's accusations? She had no idea. She was used to her community, where things progressed slowly and in sequence. Perhaps things were done differently in the English world. How would she know, after all?

Shaking slightly, she slowly walked back upstairs to her bedroom, climbing into bed. She had asked God for an answer, to lead her to decide. Perhaps, he had done just that.

But the fact remained: how on earth was she going to face David, in the morning?

***

Rachel stared out the window the next morning, breathing a sigh of relief. The blizzard was over. They were no longer stuck in the house.

She walked outside, grabbing her basket as she went. She needed to collect the eggs. Half of her hoped that David would be gone by the time she got inside. She didn't think that she could look him in the face, again.

Contradictory thoughts raced through her head, chasing each other. On the one hand, she felt anger toward him. How could he have done what he did? But on the other hand, she felt like she must have done something to provoke it. Something that she had no awareness of.

Her eyes filled with tears, again. It was better that she remain out here, amongst the hens. She didn't think that she could trust herself around anyone. She might burst into tears at the slightest thing.

The girls had not laid very many, of course. They never produced much, in winter. She could have completed the chore quickly, but she lagged.

She heard a noise, behind her. Her heart was gripped with fear. It wasn't David, was it?

But no. It was Abraham, walking up to her. "*Gutentag*," he called.

"*Gutentag*," she called back. She could feel her voice shake. She needed to get herself together.

"You are taking your time," he said, frowning as he looked in her basket. "Not many, today." He paused, looking at her. "I just wanted you to know, your friend David has left. He said he was in a hurry, and couldn't say good bye to you." Abraham frowned. "He was acting strangely, or stranger than he usually acts, at any rate."

Rachel's eyes glimmered with tears. She bit her lip. Don't say anything, she told herself fiercely.

"Rachel," Abraham said, softly. "What is wrong?"

She sat down, abruptly. Abraham sat down beside her.

"It's nothing," she said, wiping her eyes with the back of her hand. "I'm just being silly. I slept badly last night."

He said nothing, just let her catch her breath. But his eyes narrowed.

"Rachel," he said. "Look at me."

She turned her face, reluctantly, toward him.

"What did he do to you?" he whispered. "I'll go after him, this minute."

"No!" She reached out, laying a hand on his arm. He looked down at it.

"Then tell me what is wrong," he said.

"It's just a misunderstanding," she said. "David thought...that there was an expectation in our friendship. I had to tell him there wasn't. He wasn't happy – that is why he left this morning, so abruptly. He obviously didn't want to speak to me."

"What happened? Did he hurt you?" His face was dark.

She laughed, a little tremulously. "Oh, no," she whispered. "Not physically, anyway. He hurt my feelings, but that's okay. I should have known better."

"What are you talking about?" He said, frowning. "Known better than what? Rachel, the only thing that you should have known was to stay away from that man. I know you think that I don't like him just because he's English, but it's not that. I could tell what kind of man he was, straight away. He was trying to take advantage of you."

Rachel hung her head. The tears that had been threatening spilled over.

"Don't cry, Rachel," he said, gently. "I can't bear it, to see you like this."

"What can't you bear?" she cried, suddenly. "Why do you even care? You haven't been my friend in a long time, Abraham. Why should you suddenly decide what is good for me, and what isn't? Friends don't treat each other like this. Friends are there for each other, through thick and thin."

Abraham's hands balled into fists. "I couldn't watch it," he said, slowly. "I couldn't watch what you were doing. Toying with the English world. I thought you were going, Rachel. I thought you were making the decision to leave our community, and it made me so sad."

He took a deep breath. "And then, when I saw you hanging around with *him*." He spat the word, as if it was something distasteful. "I knew straight away what kind of a man he was. But you had stars in her eyes, talking about art and life away from here."

Rachel got to her feet, grabbing the basket. "Well, isn't that nice," she said. "I would never have done that to you. Friends are supposed to be there for each other, regardless of what is happening in each other's lives. But you aren't a real friend, are you, Abraham? You are one of those fair weather variety, only around when the going is good."

"How can you say that?" His voice was raised. "I have always been there for you, looking out for you when we were at school! I have been a better friend to you than most. The only time I have turned away from you was when I thought you were leaving me!"

He was panting. Rachel felt tears welling, again. What was the point of this? They couldn't communicate, anymore. They had grown so far away from each other. It was sad, but it couldn't be mended, obviously.

"The blizzard has cleared," she said. "I think you need to leave, Abraham."

She walked past him, refusing to look at him.

No, she had no idea of anything, anymore. She had lost two people who she had thought were friends. One of them she had been losing for a while, anyway; it had been a band aid she had been frightened to rip off, for fear of the pain. But in the end, she got the pain anyway. The other was a quick pain that would keep hurting, for a while at least.

There was no avoiding pain, that was obvious. You might try to dodge it, walk around it, or ignore it, but it would follow you, whether you liked it or not.

She prayed silently as she walked. She had been full of confusion about her life, and what she would do. At least now, one path was gone. She would not be keen to experience the English world, again. She was out of her depth, and besides, the incident with David had made her realise how dear her world was to her. She didn't want to lose it; not now, not ever.

She would talk to her father. She had made her decision; she wanted to be baptized into the faith.

She thought of Abraham. No, he hadn't followed her. She knew he wouldn't. He had made his choice, a long time ago. And she didn't want to be friends with someone, anyway, who couldn't accept her for herself. The good sides of her, as well as the bad.

It was all for the best.

***

Rachel sat beside her best friend Lovina. It felt good to re-connect with her. She hadn't seen her in a long time, since she had been busy with David.

The two girls were inside, next to the blazing fire. The roads had finally opened, and Christmas had come and gone. Lovina had called around to Rachel's house to deliver her Christmas present.

Rachel's eyes shone when she ripped open the small present. In her lap was a handmade crocheted rug. Rachel threw her arms around her friend.

"Thank you," she whispered, tears in her eyes. She hadn't lost all her friends.

"You're welcome," Lovina said, smiling. She had already opened Rachel's present to her, a knitted scarf. It was wound around her neck.

"You can take it off, you know," Rachel said, gesturing to the scarf. "It must be hot wearing it inside!"

The two girls laughed. Then Lovina looked at her friend. She could tell something was bothering her.

"How is David?" she asked, gently. It was as she thought. At the mere mention of the name, Rachel bristled and blushed.

"What happened, Rachel?" Lovina took her friend's hand.

"Oh," Rachel tried to smile. "We had an argument. He thought something that wasn't true about me, and didn't believe me when I told him he was wrong. It doesn't matter."

"I thought that might be the case," said Lovina, looking at her friend tenderly. "Dear Rachel, you are so shy and unsure around men. Sometimes, they misunderstand things. Especially in the English world, or so I have been told." She paused, looking at Rachel. "Have you made a decision? Do you want to stay in the faith?"

"I do," answered Rachel. It felt like a weight was lifted off her shoulders, just saying the words. She felt lighter, somehow.

Yes, the incident with David had been the catalyst, but it was more than that. God had shown her all that she stood to lose if she embraced the English world. As far as Rachel was concerned, the price was far too high to pay.

"I am so happy," said Lovina. She clutched Rachel's hands, tears in her eyes. "I don't know what I would have done without you. And I know that I am not the only one who feels that way, Rachel."

"What do you mean?"

"I am talking about Abraham." Lovina looked at her friend, gauging her reaction. "He has been so troubled, watching your forays into the English world."

Rachel scoffed. "I think you are mistaken, Lovina. Abraham doesn't care for me, any longer. He made that very clear after the blizzard. He was never a real friend."

"Rachel, how can you be so dense?" Lovina looked at her friend, her eyes widening. "It's because he is a real friend that he was so concerned! But there is more to it than that. I think he has stronger feelings for you, Rachel."

"What?" Rachel looked at her friend as if she had just started talking in another language. She shook her head, vigorously. "No, you are mistaken. If he felt that way about me, why wouldn't he have told me? And why would he just cut me off?"

"Because he was hurt, Rachel," Lovina replied. "He thought you were rejecting our faith and him, in the process. It was too much for him; he felt like he had to turn away completely." Lovina glanced sideways at Rachel. "That's what I believe, anyway."

"No, you are wrong," said Rachel, frowning.

She stood up. "I might just get a glass of water," she said. She walked to the kitchen, thinking deeply.

Lovina's words were swimming around in her brain. They made no sense to her. It was as if her world had tilted sideways. Could it be true?

And how did she feel, if it was? Abraham had been a constant in her life, as stable as the sun and the moon in the sky to her. She had assumed that he would be there, forever. It had hurt her immeasurably when he had withdrawn from her. As if the sun had dimmed, and the moon had stopped shedding its luminescence.

As if her world had stopped.

***

At least her parents were happy. That was something.

Rachel had told them her decision to join the faith, and they had been overjoyed.

"We were so worried about you," said her mother. "We thought there was a strong chance that you would join the English world." She had clasped her daughter's hands, her eyes full of tears.

Her father had nodded, pleased. "I always knew you would make the right decision," he said. "Rachel, the world is full of wonders. But your place is here, with us. I am glad that God has shown you the right path."

She was feeling a bit better about the incident with David. She accepted it for what it was, and that she had misjudged him. She had been swept away by the world he offered, for a little while. It was as simple as that.

Now that she had made her decision, everything was clear. Except, maybe, what had happened with Abraham.

She realised that she loved him. She always had. But he had turned away from her, so there was no hope for them, now. If only she had realised sooner. Maybe they might have had a chance.

Rachel walked to the end of their property, thinking deeply. She was happy that she was going to be baptised, but she was also sad. Sad for a lost love, that had never developed.

She heard a noise behind her, and turned around. The snow was still deep; although the sky was clear, she hadn't expected anyone else to be out here.

A dark figure loomed before her. She had to blink twice, thinking that she had conjured him from her imagination.

For in front of her was Abraham.

Yes, it was really him.

"Rachel." He walked toward her, not smiling. "Your mother told me you were out here, taking a walk." He paused, struggling for words. "I need to talk to you. I feel that you have misunderstood me, and I can't stop thinking about it."

She looked at him, snowflakes brushing his dark winter overcoat and black hat. Her heart swelled. If she could stand here, like this, forever, just looking at him, she would be happy.

"Abraham." She stared into his eyes. Was it possible? Were Lovina's words true?

Abraham sighed, deeply. "Will you walk with me?"

"Of course," she said.

They turned and started walking, together. She glanced at him sideways, trying to judge his mood. But he was still silent, gathering his thoughts.

Eventually, he stopped and turned.

"I know it is useless," he blurted. "But it doesn't matter to me, anymore. I have tried for so long to stop feeling this way. I know that you don't feel the same way. But I can't deny it. I have to at least tell you."

Rachel's heart stopped, just for a moment. Her breath caught on the cold wind.

"Rachel, I love you," he said, his eyes pleading. "I have loved you forever, and I will never stop loving you. I haven't told you, because I saw that you weren't ready. You needed to go off and explore the world. I was trying to give you space, to find yourself."

"Oh, Abraham," she gasped. "I had no idea. I was so hurt when you refused to be my friend, any longer. I just couldn't understand."

"It hurt me too much," he whispered, "to see you. Knowing that I loved you. And then when you started seeing David, I thought that was it. There was no chance at all." He paused, taking a deep breath. "I wanted to respect your decision. Even though I knew that he didn't deserve you."

Rachel's eyes filled with tears. "Abraham," she whispered back. "I was confused. I wasn't sure where I belonged. But I have made up my mind, now. My place is here, in our community."

He smiled, for the first time that day. It was beautiful to her. "I am so glad," he said.

"And my place is with you," she continued, facing him. "I am sorry it has taken me so long to realise it. I love you, too, Abraham. I always have, and I always will."

His smile spread wider across his face. His eyes glimmered with tears. "It is more than I hoped for. I can't tell you how many times I have dreamed of this moment." He paused. "Rachel, will you be my wife?"

The tears that had been threatening spilled over. "Oh Abraham, nothing in this world would make me happier," she breathed.

Her heart was overflowing.

It had taken her a while, to get here. To find her place in her community, and realise her love. But it had been worth it, the journey. She wouldn't take back a moment of it; not the soul searching, or the confusion. She wouldn't even take back what had happened with David.

Because it had all led her here, to this moment. As God had planned, all along.

THE END

The Amish Arrangement

Marisa Meyer

Independence was thrust upon Michelle Raber, an Amish woman from Pennsylvania, when she finally decided to take control of her life and leave an abusive life behind. Now miles away from home and family she finally managed to start over. Running her own bakery, Pearls and Swirls, she needs nothing more, especially romance. But when Eva Lapp pays her an unexpected visit with a surprising request her life is turned upside down. Required to be Eva's grandson Daniel's pretend-girlfriend, she's conflicted by the sudden rush of feelings that develop towards him, but the lie is suffocating her.

Daniel, a handsome Amish bachelor who keeps to himself has no interest in marriage or romance after the death of his father Jacob, a year after his mother Rachel passed away. But Bishop Fischer has other plans. Daniel is to ask his daughter Grace for her hand by Christmas, whether he likes it or not. Opposed to the idea, he goes along with his grandmother's plan only to realize that he's falling for Michelle Raber.

Neither of the two are particularly fond of Christmas... until now.

Chapter 1

The cheer and joy of the season was palpable. Christmas was a few weeks away and everywhere in the small town of Loudonville, shops were decorated with Christmas trees and decorations. Everywhere except at Swirls and Pearls. Here in the quaint little bakery, the only sign of Christmas was the sweet aroma of freshly backed Christmas cakes and minced pies that teased the senses of many passing tourists and locals, leaving Michelle with hardly any time for herself. But she dared not complain. It was good for business and worth every penny. She had bills to pay and running a bakery was not cheap. It had been two years since she arrived at Loudonville and it had been her only chance for a fresh start, far away from Caleb and his violent temper. It had taken her three years, two months and half a week, to the day, with a lot of convincing from her close friends and family to make the move and leave him behind. Not that she needed convincing. After ending up in hospital with a fractured jaw, two broken ribs and a lie that she had fallen, she had no choice. Her mother and sister along with her best friend Abigail convinced her to run away and never look back. No contact and no letters, not even a hint. They all had known what Caleb was capable of. As an upstanding man in Lancaster County and one of the richest too, Caleb had aimed to make her his wife. It all started out fine, he courted her, treated her well until it was time to set a date for a wedding. That's when things took a turn for the worst. Caleb had a jealous streak, and she was not allowed to work or talk to any other man. It had been after she ended up in hospital that her mother helped her to run away. She had given Michelle all her savings to start over.

Michelle rolled the bread dough in the bowl and kneaded it vigorously. Keeping busy at Swirls and Pearls had kept her mind from wandering back home and in the midst of travesty and sorrow, she had found that spark of hope. She could bake to her heart's content. See kids lick their fingers after a serving of sugary cinnamon sugar donuts and lose herself in decorating birthday and wedding cakes. She was content.

She swiped a strand of hair away from her brow with the back of her hand covered in dough and straightened her back.

"Michelle, I have an order for four dozen bagels from Mr. Morris."

Michelle smiled at her assistant Mary, who had been working for her since she opened the bakery. Mary was a sweet young girl, with curly blonde hair and sky blue eyes who never failed to smile. It was her bubbly personality that often made this place come alive. And even as an Englischer she respected Michelle.

"When does he need it for?"

"Tomorrow morning, he said he'll be here just after nine."

"Are you serious?"

Mr. Morris who owned the coffee shop two blocks down was one of her regular clients. She supplied him with many delicacies such as flavoured bagels. She didn't mind, but he had the habit to drop an order on her on the last minute, leaving her to work till late at night to ensure it was ready for when he collected.

"Should I tell him to pick it up at twelve, rather?"

"No, it's fine," said Michelle and looked at the clock on the wall. "I'll have it ready."

Mary gave a chuckle and shook her head. "You need to talk to him about these last minute orders, I bet you if he knew you worked until midnight just to keep him happy, he won't take such liberties."

"Perhaps, but I really do not mind. It keeps me busy. Idle hands are the devils playground."

Mary laughed, "The devil won't bother wasting his time in Loudonville, there's nothing here to do as it is."

Michelle didn't respond, she let Mary believe whatever she wanted, but in her experience, it didn't take a big city to lure out the wickedness of a deranged jealous man.

The doorbell to the entrance jingled and an elderly Amish woman entered the bakery. Michelle recognized Mrs Lapp instantly. She had brought the bakery from her son Jacob Lapp a year ago after he had lost his wife to a terminal illness. Jacob was so heartbroken; he wanted nothing that reminded him of his beloved Rachel.

"Mrs Lapp, what a pleasant surprise, *wie bischt du heit*?" Michelle greeted and wiped her hands clean from the sticky dough.

"Hello Michelle," the elderly woman mumbled. "I'm *gut ya,* I like what you've done to the bakery."

Michelle looked around her. She had done little to change it. It still had the same Amish charm as when she first walked in. She replaced the curtains to the storefront though and added a few new paintings to the walls. But the wicker baskets used for the bread and rolls, and the old charm cane furniture was all still there.

"Thank you Mrs Lapp, I tried to keep the store exactly as it was when Jacob owned it. I only changed the name and added a little to the interior décor."

"Please call me Eva," she said averting her gaze and clearing her throat. "A word, if we may?"

Michelle frowned. Eva looked sad, but how would that have anything to do with her or Pearls and Swirls. She asked Mary to make some tea and led Eva to the small table in the corner of the bakery near the window.

"Here sit down; can I offer you any tea?"

Eva shook her head, ringing her hands in front of her.

"Michelle, I wouldn't come here if I didn't think it absolutely necessary."

"What is it Eva?" she whispered and cupped Eva's hand.

"Jacob passed away two weeks ago."

Michelle held back a gasp and squeezed Eva's hands. "That's just terrible, I'm so sorry for your loss, he was a *gut* man."

Eva dabbed a stray tear with the corner of her apron and closed her eyes.

"*Het is Gods wil.*"

The Amish never questioned God's will, not even in the grimmest times. Whatever happened or whatever tragedy struck, they accepted it as the will of God. Having grown up in an Amish home she related to that concept once upon a time. But the older and the wiser she became the more questions she had in relation to the belief that everything was His will. Surely he wouldn't want a woman to be beaten to a pulp and leave her for dead? She shook the thought from her mind. This was not about her, this was about Eva.

"So what is it I can do for you?" she finally asked.

Eva shifted in her chair and glanced out the window. "My nephew Daniel, Jacob's son, is not doing very well and the Bishop feels he should take a wife."

Jacob had a son? This was news to her. Then again, she had never known him all that well. She only ever dealt with Jacob during the transfer of the store into her name and although he was a kind man, he hardly ever spoke of his family.

"I can understand how he must feel," she whispered. "But I don't understand what this has to do with me."

"It is *Chrischdaag* in two weeks, and Bishop Fischer insists that he should choose a wife by then or he would insist that Daniel marries his daughter Grace."

Michelle swallowed, and a puzzled frown drew her brows together, Eva was not making any sense. She sat back against the chair and regarded Eva with curiosity.

"I don't know where else to turn. You see, Abel is away at his Rumspringa and I know that he fancies Grace, but he will only be back after *Chrischdaag*. But it might be too late."

Michelle had a terrible feeling about this, but she waited for Eva to continue.

"I was wondering if you could pose as um..."

"His girlfriend?!" Michelle spluttered. "Eva, I don't even know Daniel. You can't expect me to lie."

"Michelle, please. I dreaded coming here and asking this of you, but Daniel would be so unhappy if he is forced to marry. You only need to pretend until Abel is back and Grace's attention is diverted."

That was straight to the point, she thought. But how could she lie like that, and how would she even be able to pull it off?

"Eva, I would really love to help your nephew..."

"Oh I knew you would help," Eva interrupted and tapped on the window.

"What I mean to say is that..." she glanced out the window and her words fell silent as a young handsome man came walking towards the bakery. He was tall and muscular with short brown hair and unlike most of the Amish men she'd seen in town, he had no facial hair. But the way the muscle in his jaw jumped involuntarily was a sure sign that he was frustrated.

Eva jumped to her feet and rushed to the door to take her nephews' hand and Michelle followed. Eva hadn't given her time to explain that she can't help Daniel, but now, with him standing in front of her and the look of utter gratefulness in Eva's eyes, she couldn't bring herself to turn him away.

"Daniel this is Michelle, the girl I was telling you about."

"*Grossmammi!*" Daniel muttered under his breath and uttered a quiet, "Hello."

"Hello Daniel, I'm so sorry for your loss," said Michelle, awkwardly clasping her hands in front of her, not quite sure what else to say.

For the first time he looked at her, and the intensity of his gaze jolted her. His eyes were brown, like dark chocolate, but not sweet, more like rich unsweetened cacao. Losing his *Daed* must be very hard on him and on top of that he was staring down a barrel of a gun, being force to pick a woman to marry. The silence that passed between them felt like an eternity and it was Eva who spoke again.

"Daniel, Michelle has offered to help you with the situation and by the time Abel returns, Bishop Fischer will have no choice but to honour his daughter's wishes and allow her to marry Abel."

She was sure she saw anger flash in Daniel's eyes. He leaned in and muttered something in his grandmother's ear. Eva patted his hand and although her smile never reached her eyes, the corners of her mouth turned up and she turned her attention back to Michelle.

"This is our secret all you have to do is take Michelle to service and visit her. You can't marry Grace."

Michelle nodded and smiled at Daniel, but he averted his gaze instead and turned to head back to the buggy.

"I don't think he's in agreement with this," she said, biting her lip, "Maybe it will be better if he just tells Bishop Fischer how he feels?"

"Daniel does not love Grace, and I cannot bear to see him unhappy. He's a gut man and he will treat you well."

It's not me I'm worried about, she thought as Eva walked down the few steps and crossed the road to join her grandson.

"What was that all about?" Mary asked as she came to stand next to her.

"It is complicated."

Mary sniffed and crossed her arms. "Wanna talk about it?"

"No."

Michelle turned and went back inside, her mind swirling with questions. Why on earth did Eva pick her out of all the other women in Loudonville to be her grandson's pretend girlfriend?

Chapter 2

The small flickering flame from the oil lamp was the only source of light in living room where Daniel sat contemplating life. He had so many questions with no real answers. He should have taken a wife earlier in life while his parents were still alive, but now with them both having passed on, things were grim. Bishop Fischer had been insisting he takes a wife to produce a namesake for his family, yet, he didn't see Grace as someone he would spend the rest of his life with. She was a deluded soul and he couldn't help but compare her to the vain self-centred Scarlet O'Hara from Gone with the wind. Yes, he had a few books stacked under his bed, which he read from time to time. Something he had been hiding from the community and his parents since his first discovery of Hamlet. If Bishop Fischer or Grace ever found out he was reading worldly books, he would certainly be shunned, but he didn't care. He was an inquisitive soul and as time passed, he couldn't help the need for knowledge. If he had it his way, he would have stayed away when he went on his first Rumspringa but his loyalty to his family brought him back and now he felt obligated to do the right thing. But what was the right thing?

Daniel put the latest book he'd been reading in the coffer and pushed it back under his bed then laid down and stared up at the ceiling. His *grossmammi* was a work of art. Never in his wildest dreams would he have thought her to be so determined. She knew he didn't like Grace, and she knew if he ended up marrying her, he would be miserable, but setting him up with a complete stranger was not the answer. And to make matters worse, she was beautiful too. Michelle Raber, the woman he had always admired from afar. When his mother died a year ago, and his father could no longer cope with the bakery, he had sold it to her. Daniel never met with her, but he knew of her.

He draped his arm over his eyes and sighed, but out of the blue and image of the young woman from the bakery appeared before him. Now having met her in person he couldn't help but wonder about her.

She was friendly and although she runs her own business, she didn't seem proud. In fact she was the complete opposite of Grace and he could discern that in a matter of five minutes. If Grace had owned that bakery she would do all the work herself, greed and status was far more important to her than having to be bothered with helpers, but she was cunning in her own way. Her father praised her for her humbleness but he could see right through her.

Chapter 3

The orders were piling up and Michelle and Mary had been working late every night. This time of the year was bound to be busier than normal. Tourists visited the small town daily in the dozens and they all stopped at Swirls and Pearls. But even though things were busy, Michelle's mind was elsewhere. Daniel. Only two days ago, she had involuntarily signed up to be a pretend girlfriend to him, on request of his grandmother. And although she hadn't seen him since, she anticipated his eventual appearance sooner or later. Had it not been for Mary she wouldn't have been able to cope.

She glanced up at the cuckoo clock with is brilliant bright green and red colours as if it could tell the time, but it was more out of habit though. The clock had been a part of the bakery since she took ownership, but it has never worked. But she suspected it was nearly 4 pm and time to head on home. There was a sing this evening, but she wasn't in the mood to join, she was far too exhausted.

"Michelle, you have a visitor," Mary said as she poked her head into the kitchen.

"Who is it?" she asked as stacked the freshly backed ginger bread biscuits on the tray.

"It's that guy you met the other day."

Michelle turned and bumped the tray nearly dumping all the cookies on the ground. "Daniel?"

"Yeah that would be him." Mary went to push the tray back on to the table and scooped up one of the broken biscuits. "He's a very serious looking fellow. What would he want with you?"

Michelle sighed and reached for a rag to wipe her hands clean. "It's a long story."

She didn't wait for Mary to interrogate her any further and walked out of the kitchen.

"Good afternoon Daniel," she said feeling slightly breathless.

How was it even possible for her body to react this way towards a man she hardly knew? Suddenly she was all too aware of her own appearance. She could feel the crusted batter stuck on her cheek and the caked cookie dough under her finger nails. She must look aghast, she thought. The least he could have done was to warn her he would show up.

"Hello," he said holding a box in his hand. "I brought you something."

Surprised she looked at the box in his hand. "What is it?"

He held it out to her, and she accepted it with a slight flutter of her heart. When she opened it, it was an almost exact replica of the cuckoo clock against the wall, the only difference being the colours. Instead of red and green it was red and yellow with white daisies painted on the roof. But why would he give her a gift? They weren't a couple, not a real couple anyway.

"I can't accept this," she whispered and held the box out for him to take.

"Why not?"

"Daniel it's a gift, you shouldn't be giving me gifts when we both know that this arrangement is only for show."

He smiled a genuine smile that caused the laughing lines next to his eyes to scrunch up and made her heart do cart wheels.

"It's not a gift, its payment. You're helping me and I am returning the favor." He nodded with his head towards the clock on the wall. "My *daed* broke that one, after my *maemm* died. It's of no use."

She glanced up at the clock and then down at the one in the box. She knew better than to accept it, but he had a point. If she looked at it as payment, what harm was there in her accepting it?

"*Goed, dank u,*" she whispered and hugged the box to her. "I will put it up tomorrow, do you want to take that one with you?"

"No, it's yours."

An awkward silence passed between them and then Daniel took his hat off. "Will you join me for the sing this evening?"

It starts! Michelle thought nervously. How was she going to uphold the pretence knowing it was a blatant lie? But the way he looked at her was with such sincerity she could hardly catch her breath. Two weeks to Christmas that was all. She forced a smile and nodded.

"Ya, I will be ready at six."

"Gut."

And with that Daniel turned and left.

"Is that what I think it is?" Mary asked as she popped up from behind the counter.

"What?"

"Did Daniel just give you a gift?"

As an Englischer working for an Amish woman, Mary knew all too well what it meant when a man gives a woman a gift. Michelle had been determined to teach Mary about their ways and the laws of their religion, hoping that Mary would someday find grace and peace amongst them.

"Oh no, no—it's not a gift." Michelle blurted and deposited it on the counter.

"It looks like a gift to me." Mary grinned.

"Well it isn't. He's trading the clock for the broken one on the wall which belonged to his family."

Forgive me God, she prayed silently. Another lie upon another lie, soon enough the truth was bound to catch up with her, she thought.

"I see, well why didn't he just take it then?"

Frustrated with the questions, Michelle stalked to the door and closed it, flipping the closed sign on the glass pane.

"Because we were closing and he can come back tomorrow to take it."

The smile on Mary's face was one of amusement, and Michelle knew her employee and Englisch friend didn't believe one word.

Mary peeked in the box on the counter and gasped, "Did he make this?"

"You should go on home now," Michelle muttered, "Remember we are staring an hour early tomorrow."

The young girl smiled and nodded before walking to the back. Michelle sighed and leaned with her hip against the counter. Once this whole thing was over, she would resign herself to being a spinster. She wasn't interested in marriage or any relationship for that matter, not after all she had to endure with Caleb. Lucky she was stronger now and although she was Daniel's pretend girlfriend, he had no hold on her.

Chapter 4

It was the Sunday before Christmas, Daniel and Michelle had kept up the appearance of being a happy couple. The first time they were seen together in public was at the Thursday evening Sing, and at first the puzzled look from others made her uncomfortable, but Daniel had set her mind at ease. He never left her side and made sure she was not left on her own for anyone to pester her. Eva on the other hand treated her like a daughter, showering her with simple gifts like knitted blankets and even a new dress. As for Grace, she didn't fail to show her utter distaste with this agreement. Eva had reassured her that Grace was in love with Abel, and that she was only doing what the Bishop expected, so her behaviour towards her and Daniel was strange to say the least.

"Michelle."

A cold shiver ran up her spine and settled at the base of her neck. Grace had finally decided to confront her. She turned around slowly only to be face to face with her soon to be nemesis and Bishop Fischer.

"Hello Bishop Fisher, hello Grace," she said plastering a smile on her face.

"I see you and Daniel are quite acquainted?" The Bishop said stoically.

"Daniel is a good man."

"That he is," Grace chirped up, "I'm just wondering how the two of you met?"

Shoot! Grace thought in panic, neither of them ever discussed the details of their supposed status and how they came to be so close. She dug into the recesses of her mind to find a plausible reasoning.

"Well, we, I mean I met him when I bought the bakery from Jacob and we've been acquaintances since then."

"Yet you only made it official now, how convenient."

The bitterness rolled off of Grace's tongue like poison Ivy. Michelle glanced passed them trying to locate Daniel and hoping he could come to her rescue.

"You know how these things are, there's no use rushing into something too serious in such a short span of time."

"Perhaps, where you come from, but here we do things differently," the Bishops muttered under his breath. "Daniel is promised to Grace, and I think it's time you step aside."

"Hallo Bishop. Grace." Daniel appeared out of nowhere, nodding his head at the two and then casually took Michelle's hand in his. "The service was gut ya?"

She lowered her eyes, not wanting to look at Grace and the Bishop, fearing that they may see the guilt reflecting in her eyes.

"Das was gut. Daniel," the Bishop started, "What is the meaning of this relationship between the two of you?"

Talk about being direct, Michelle though but Daniel squeezed her and reassuringly.

"I don't know what you mean Bishop? We're in love."

"Daniel! How could you be so brazen? You were promised to me." Grace said, breaching on a temper tantrum.

"I know of no such thing Grace, a promise could not have been made without me knowing."

Michelle dared to look up. The Bishop's lips were drawn in a tight line and Grace's cheeks were flushed.

"You've bundled!" she cried out.

"Grace! You cannot go around making such accusations," her father said warningly.

"It's not an accusation, I've seen them. This witch had visited Daniel at his home with no one present."

Michelle's eyes grew as wide as saucers. "I have done no such thing Grace!"

"Lies, you have. He's even given you a gift!"

"And so?" Daniel muttered, "A gift well deserved. I'm in love with her and that's the end of it, I have made no promise to you."

"You're a fool!" Grace ground out, spun around and ran to her father's buggy.

"This is not the last of it Daniel, you must confess your sins, and you," he said directing his gaze to Michelle. "If you do not confess your sins and put an end to the debacle you call a relationship, you will face shunning."

His words carried an air of finality to them. And neither Daniel nor Michelle spoke, but the rest of the community or those left after the service looked upon them as if they were already shunned.

"How could she lie so blatantly?" Michelle whispered as Daniel took her hand and walked her to his buggy.

"Because she is not getting her way," he simply said.

"But your *grossmammi* told me she is in love with Abel, why would she be mad?"

Daniel helped her into the buggy and walked around to get in, and without a word he set off. They rode in silence until they reached his house. He should feel bad for putting her in this situation, in reality he should not have allowed his *grossmammi* to manipulate the situation like this, but after thinking it through he too realized that this was the only way he could ensure that he did not end up with Grace. Besides, he had enjoyed Michelle's company. Somehow between meeting her at the bakery, giving her a new cuckoo clock and taking her to the sing, he had fallen for her. She was a beautiful chaste woman with a kind heart. While time was on his side, he had also made contact with her family in Pennsylvania. Unlike the Swartzentruber one of the oldest and most conservative orders, who did not believe in technology, her family was from the Troyer order, and he too had considered that the ways he was led to believe wasn't the alpha and omega of holy living. He'd been a searcher all his life, even when his parents were both alive. But since he met Michelle, his eyes had been opened.

"Why are you bringing me to your house?"

"I want to show you something."

"But the people will gossip and Bishop Fischer will use any excuse to shun us."

"Then so be it, we're not doing anything wrong. Come."

He took her hand and led her down the small gravel path past the house towards the barn and had to slow his steps for her to keep up.

When they finally reached the barn, he pushed open the heavy doors and led her inside.

"Your mother is a lovely woman, very protective."

"You've met my mother?" she asked puzzled.

"No, but we have spoken on the telephone."

"When... why?" she asked and he could sense the fear in the tone of her voice.

"Not to worry Michelle, Caleb doesn't know, and he's no threat to you."

When Michelle's mother told him about Caleb and how ill he treated her, he was shocked; he had to do everything in his power not to go and teach him a lesson, but he knew God will be her advocate and Caleb will pay for his transgressions in God's way. But having learned more about her, he wanted her to experience life and love as it should be, starting with a true gift he had been working on for her.

They entered the barn, and he took her to the work bench at the back against the wall.

"Close your eyes."

She looked at him and frowned.

"Close your eyes; I have a surprise for you."

She hesitantly placed her hands over her eyes and when he was sure she was not peeking, he unveiled his gift.

"You can look now."

She opened her eyes and her hand instantly flew to her mouth and a soft gasp escaped her.

"I thought this would help you in the bakery. It's a rotary mixer."

She looked at the gift, then at him, then back at the gift standing on the work bench. Then suddenly her eyes shot full of tears and she fled the barn.

"Michelle wait!" he called after her but she continued to run, stumbling as she did.

Perplexed by her reaction he eventually stopped and let her be. Maybe he had made a mistake to think there could be anything between them. He went into this arrangement level headed as any sane bachelor would, but he had lost the plot. This was a temporary arrangement only and he should have accepted it as such.

With a heavy heart he turned around and headed to the house.

Chapter 5

Christmas morning arrived like a thief in the night, and Michelle's heart was torn. Ever since the day Daniel had unveiled the gift he had made her she had been in hiding. And it had nothing to do with the gift, it had everything to do with the fact she had promised herself not to fall in love again. But Daniel had made it practically impossible for her. He was the total opposite of Caleb, but she couldn't trust it to last. Every man had the best of intentions initially, but a truth was revealed to her and she had to protect her heart at all costs, no matter how much it hurt.

She shuffled tiredly to the kitchen to make tea, through the window she could see people making their way to church for the Christmas service. The atmosphere on the outside, compared to her home was worlds apart. She scanned the small crowd of people, and spotting Eva she instantly looked for Daniel, but he was nowhere in sight. She should really put a stop to this madness once and for all. She rushed to her room and got dressed and headed out to the church adamant to talk to Eva and put an end to this arrangement. When she arrived, everyone had taken their seats in the hall, and Bishop Fischer was standing on the podium, his head bowed in silent prayer. Right in the front row sat Grace, her head held high, almost defiantly so and next to her a young gentleman with longish blonde hair. Eva patted the seat next to her,

"Come sit."

Michelle scooted in and sat next to Eva. "I can't do this anymore," she whispered.

"Do what dear?"

"This lie, it's not right."

"Is it really a lie?"

Eva's question was simple, but it bore into Michelle's soul and realisation swept over her like river, stripping her of the conviction and guilt she'd been haunted with for the past few days.

"Is that Abel?" she asked instead of answer Eva.

"Ya, a handsome fellow and he is a good match for Grace, much better suited than my Daniel."

"Where is he?"

"He'll be here soon."

The service started and both of them sat quietly while Bishop Fischer continued with the sermon. He read the infamous passage from the bible Luke 2:1-20 proclaiming the wondrous birth of Jesus Christ. She should pay attention to the sermon but she couldn't. She kept looking over her shoulder for a sign any sign of Daniel and when the sermon had finally come to an end, she couldn't wait to get out.

"Michelle!" Eva called after her just as she exited the hall.

With a heavy sigh, she turned around and waited for Eva.

"My heart is heavy Eva," she admitted. "Daniel deserves to find a good wife, not a pretend girlfriend. He's a good, good man."

Eva smiled softly and took her by the hand. "So he is, he deserves a woman who would honour him but above all love and cherish him, a woman who fears God."

"Exactly!" Michelle exclaimed, "This lie we've been upholding is dishonourable to both God and Daniel, it has to end."

The elderly woman stopped and turned to face Michelle, her grey eyes seemingly searching.

"Then end it, go now and tell him it's over. Grace has found her half and Bishop Fischer is pleased."

She let out a breath, but the sigh of relief was only temporary. The realisation that her pretend courtship would come to an end left her empty and bare. Even though she knew what she had to do, she could never bring herself to do so. She parted ways with Eva, but instead of going home she headed to the fields, she needed to clear her mind and figure out why she was so confused.

Daniel had deliberately decided not to attend the service that morning. He couldn't. Michelle's rejection of his gift had left him vulnerable and right now facing her was too difficult. He had fallen for her, against his better judgement, and just because he acted on his feelings he had ruined the one good thing that came from this arrangement. He should have waited, should have been patient until he was certain she was ready. As he sat on his porch, he watched as other town folk headed home from the service. In the distance he noticed his *grossmammi* talking to Michelle and his heart cramped in his chest. Their entire friendship had been built on a lie. Had he gotten to know her earlier, they may have had something good, but instead he avoided her, like he avoided all other women. But she was the first one to make him feel whole again, despite the arrangement they had. When he had given her the cuckoo clock, he could see the shimmer of appreciated and adoration in her eyes, even though she tried to hide it. When he took her to the sing, he felt as if the empty part of him was slowly filling up with love and adoration. And now, on the precipice of truth, he would forever lose her. He set his carving knife aside and again looked towards the church. His aunt was alone now and then he spotted her walking across the field, his earlier uncertainty suddenly gone and in its place determination. Within minutes he crossed the field towards her and when he reached her, he heard the soft sobs that struck his heart like a sharp knife.

"Michelle?" he whispered.

She had spotted him coming her way long before he reached her, and her insides were a mess. As much as she wanted to make an end to the arrangement she couldn't bring herself to utter the words.

"Daniel," she breathed and turned to face him as she wiped the tears from her eyes.

"I feel I need to apologize for the situation I have put you in."

She looked down and shook her head, "I should never have agreed to it, your *grossmammi* was just trying to help and I couldn't say no to her please."

Daniel stepped closer, "She can be very persuasive, I should not have allowed her to go this far."

"I saw Grace and Abel."

Why she felt the need to mention that was beyond her, but she had no idea what else to say. Maybe it was out of justification more than anything. She felt the need to justify her actions, not only to him but to herself.

"I know. He arrived yesterday."

"You knew, and you didn't tell me?" she asked in disbelief.

He shook his head and frowned, picking on a stem of grass. "I couldn't, I... in all honesty, the truth is that I didn't want to tell you."

"But why Daniel, we've been living a lie and everyone has expectations for us, even Mary."

He met her gaze with an intensity that seared her soul. "Is it really a lie?"

It's the second time she's heard the same question, and it's the same question she had been plagued with. All this time she was convinced that her heart and her mind was deceiving her, and now Daniel was feeding that lie.

"Of course it's a lie, what else could it be? We lied to Bishop Fischer, we lied to Grace, heavens, we lied to everyone even to ourselves," she blurted out.

Daniel stepped closer and reached to brush a strand of hair from her cheek and smiled.

"It may have started out as one, but I think there was a greater purpose to this so called lie. The first time I saw you were when you met with my *daed*, it was just after my *maemm's* funeral. I was broken then, I love my parents. But when I saw you I saw hope and peace, but it was my pride that kept me from saying anything. I admired you from afar, lying to myself and convincing myself that I didn't care, but you see Michelle, I do care. I care so much for you. The past two weeks had been hell, if I may say so, but it's brought me to you."

Michelle was speechless, this was the last thing she had expected to hear, but hearing those words were like medicine to a wound. Her eyes shot full of tears and her chin wobbled. Could this be real?

"Why didn't you just tell me?"

"I was afraid. I watched my daed fade away after my *maemm* passed, and I couldn't imagine the agony and pain he must have felt, losing the only woman he had ever loved. And knowing that time would come for me some day, I was too scared to commit to love. But then I realized, that death leaves a heart ache that no one can heal, but love leaves a memory that cannot be stolen."

A sob escaped her, and she covered her face as Daniel pulled her into his arms.

"The only lie here is the lie that we don't belong together," he whispered and then pressed his lips against her forehead and wiped her tears with the pads of his thumbs.

"Oh Daniel, the thought of losing you was unbearable, I don't want to live a lie anymore. I'm in love you," she cried as she held on to him.

"And I'm in love with you."

She smiled softly and whispered, "This is the best Christmas ever."

Rosemary and Sawdust

Terri Downes

Rosemary and Sawdust

Paul looked in the box again, as though the key might have appeared there in the last two minutes. He glanced back down at the instructions on his phone. *Will leave front door key in wood box on left side of porch. Let me know how it goes, Derek*

Paul huffed a sigh. Derek had never been the most reliable in the family, and Paul had had his doubts about letting him take point in terms of checking out their uncle's property. He had tried to convince him that it would be easier if he, Paul, were to handle everything with the will executors, as he was the one who would who had actually inherited the place. But Derek lived closer, and had been to the house before.

Not that it helped much, thought Paul.

The wood box had not even been where he said it was, it was on the other side of the porch. And the building was not as he had described it. It was much smaller that Derek had indicated, though admittedly in better repair, with a white clapboard front and low eaves.

Paul wished he had been able to come up here while his uncle had still been alive. He had felt terrible when he had found out that he had been left the house – Uncle Ethan had always been inviting him up on weekends, telling him it would be good for him to get away from it all, that they could take the kind of fishing trips Paul had loved as a young boy – but Paul had been busy. And now all he had left was the house, to fix up and sell to someone who had not even known his uncle.

Looking back up at the house, he hoped that he would be able to sell it. This was not exactly a hub for people buying holiday homes. It was mostly farmland, and the only tourists were the ones interested in the local Amish people. But the house would probably need to be sold as a holiday home if he were to turn the kind of profit he was hoping. He had asked the guys from work if they would be willing to do the house on speculation, for a percentage of the sale afterward, and he knew they would only be willing if the house was promising. The realtor he had spoken to had said he would need a lot of details for an assessment price, and he would need them by the end of the day.

Paul glanced from his watch to where the sun had slowly started to sink. He did not have signal here; he did not have time to go find a place to call Derek and figure out what he had done with the key, if he even remembered.

Time to get creative.

Paul headed to the side of the house, where he had seen – yes, there it was. An old tree, gnarled and bent, with a heavy, twisted trunk, leaning almost all the way over to the house. The branches started low enough to grab onto, and they looked pretty sturdy. He had already tried the lower story windows when he had realized the key was not where it should have been, but they had all been latched, and he was not willing to pay for a broken pane of glass this early on in the proceedings. But the upper story windows had been left ajar, presumably by Derek, to let in a whiff of breeze.

The house probably needs it, thought Paul, as he hoisted himself up into the tree. It was the height of summer, and the air was curdled with humidity. His shirt had started to stick to him just from the fifteen minutes he had spent outside of his car.

Still, he thought, pulling his weight up further and steadying his foot in a forked part of the trunk, the air smelled nice when it was all heavy like this. He had even rolled down the windows as he had reached the last part of his journey, which he almost never did, drinking in the scent of sun-baked grass and earth. And here, it smelled like his uncle had been growing some nice plants. Something herby and fragrant, the smell rising in the heat. And then there were the pear trees in the front, under which he had parked. He had been tempted to pick one, but he had no time for snacking.

Reaching the height he wanted, Paul slid his weight out onto a branch which gave him the best access to a window, holding onto a higher spot with one hand to keep his balance. He felt his weight pushing down, and hoped it would hold. Perhaps if he –

"Can I help you with something?"

The voice came not from the ground, but from somewhere level with Paul's ear.

He jumped in fright and lost his grip on the branch, falling forward. He flailed for a moment, scrabbling against the wall until his fingers found purchase on the windowsill he had been attempting to reach. He gripped it hard and hung there, weight stretched between the tree and the windowsill, trying to catch his breath.

"Are you all right?"said the voice that had caught him off guard.

Paul craned his neck to look upwards. The window to the right of the one he had been aiming for had been opened all the way, and a face was looking out of it. A warm, sun-browned face, spattered with freckles, framed with dark hair and some kind of hat. Frowning.

Paul would have liked to imagine that the face was frowning because of his predicament, perhaps from concern, but he was having a very unpleasant realization.

"Uh..." he said slowly, trying not to pant. "Is this your house?"

"Yes," said the woman. "Whose did you think it was?"

Paul winced. "Um. I sort of thought it was mine."

The woman raised an eyebrow. "That seems an odd mistake to make."

"Yes, yes it was..." Paul felt his palms becoming slick with sweat, and tried not to panic. "I'm very sorry about this. But, uh, could I explain properly when I'm back on the ground?"

"Oh, yes."

The woman leaned out of the window to get a better look, and Paul finally saw what she was wearing. A white cap with string ties, and a dress and apron that looked like they were out of period drama. Either she was going to a costume party, or –

"You're Amish," he said.

"Yes," said the woman, which Paul supposed was all the response such an obvious comment deserved.

"You look like you need help," said the woman.

Paul nodded. "Is your husband home?"

"No," said the woman, turning back into the house. "Beth!" she called.

Light footsteps could be heard, and a child's voice speaking in an unknown language. Pennsylvania Dutch, Paul assumed. After a brief conference which Paul could not understand, a young girl of about six or so poked her head out of the window.

She surveyed Paul critically for a moment.

"Take your left foot and slide it back up the branch," she said.

Paul blinked, then did as she said.

"There's another branch right up above you," said the girl. "Push yourself away, hard as you can, reach up and grab on."

Paul took a deep breath and pushed away from the house with both hands, keeping his weight on his left foot. He reached up and managed to grasp the branch as directed.

"Thanks," he gasped.

"You're welcome," said the girl, before disappearing from the window.

"She knows more about tree climbing than I do," said the woman, before disappearing after her daughter.

Paul sort of hoped that his rescuers would just stay in the house and allow him to make good his escape, but they appeared on the porch as he reached the front yard.

The woman looked to be in her mid twenties, dressed in black and white. Her daughter looked like a miniature version of her mother, complete with freckles and a little hat of her own.

Paul tried to explain what had happened.

"It was the GPS," he said, "I typed in Oak Crest and it sent me here."

"Oak Crest is over the hill," said the girl, Beth, pointing. "What's a GPS?"

"Oh," said Paul, "it's... like a map. It gives you directions. The wrong ones, in this case."

He turned back to the woman. "I really am sorry. I should have made certain, but I was in a hurry. I'm supposed to be selling my uncle's house, and the realtor's expecting photos of it..." he looked back at his watch, "within the hour."

The woman nodded, and made a move to start walking Paul back his car. Paul took the hint and scurried after her, wishing he did not feel so flustered. How the woman remained looking as cool and unruffled as she did, he had no idea. She must have been shocked when she had seen him there; he might have been trying to rob the place for all she knew.

As she walked, the woman gave him directions to Oak Crest.

After Paul shut the door of his car, which was thankfully still a little cool inside, he rolled down the window.

"I'm sorry," he said again. "Um – your husband – " he added, thinking he should also send an apology to the farmer for scaring his wife. But the woman shook her head.

"I'm a widow," she said quietly.

Paul's insides gave a jolt, and he clapped a hand to his head. "I'm sorry," he said, for what felt like the thousandth time in the last minute. "Really – oh, shoot, I'm sorry – "

The woman raised her hands as though to stem the tide of apology. She looked at Paul as her daughter had done, as though she were trying to work something out. She was quite small, Paul saw, compact and wiry, with a heart-shaped face. Her eyes were a deep, searching brown.

"Take a breath," she said.

"...I'm sorry?"

"Take a couple of deep breaths."

She stepped around the car toward the fence. Paul took a few deep breaths. He felt his heart begin to slow a little.

The woman reappeared, and held out a pear. Paul was not sure what else to do, so he took it. It was warm from the sun, and still had a leaf on the stem.

"Eat that," she said. "You look a little jittery." Then she turned and walked back to the house.

Paul placed the pear carefully on the passenger seat and drove off, glancing in the rear view mirror just before he turned the corner of the lane. The woman and her daughter were standing on the porch, looking out after him.

The Oak Crest house was a ten minute drive away. It was exactly how Derek had described it: a grand old wreck, with large creaking spaces and ancient fittings. It, too, was covered with whitewashed clapboard, but its veranda was warped with weather, and the some of the screens were torn.

Most of it would be easy, Paul thought, as he walked about the place snapping pictures. Sanding, painting, that sort of thing. There were no real structural issues, even the plumbing looked good at a glance, though the bathroom fittings were in his uncle's preferred 70s aesthetic and would need to be switched out with something more trendy.

The only real problem spot was the kitchen, with its dilapidated counters and cabinets and rusty sink. Paul knew that a good sale needed a good kitchen; half the jobs he and his boys took were for kitchens that were only being updated for resale value. Usually they would never even be used by the people who ordered them, but would be there for the next owners, who would then get further remodeling done when they needed to resell themselves.

Paul had always hated such transactions, knowing the work that was put in was seen only as something to increase profits; yet here he was, about to do the exact same thing. He sighed, and wandered outside into the garden, trying to find a spot with strong enough signal to send his photos to the realtor. He eventually found a place that afforded a few bars, next to the crumbling remains of a dividing wall in the back garden. It still looked as though the photos would take a few minutes, so he left his phone on top of the wall and headed back to the car. He grabbed the pear from where he had left it and went and sat on the back porch of the house, looking out at the messy garden. The earth smelled rich in the heat, though not half so good as whatever the Amish woman had been growing. That had really been something. He wondered what it was...

He wondered, too, how she had known that he had needed to eat something. He was jittery, having not had anything but coffee since breakfast, and the pear would be just the sugar kick he needed. He bit into its meltingly soft flesh and licked a bead of juice from his lip.

Oh, well, he thought. *It's not as though I'm ever going to see her again.* He finished the pear and forced himself back to his feet, going to stand by his phone as though he could increase the signal strength by staring at the thing.

—

"Dude, where are you?"

"I'm coming, I got stuck behind a tractor for a couple of miles."

Paul tried to force himself not to speed around the bends of the little country road.

"Well, we've gotta head, man, we've got another delivery to make by three. Can't we just leave the stuff here?"

Paul sighed. This was the problem calling in favors, no-one wanted to do more than they had to. It was another scorching day, and he did not relish the idea of hauling the delivery of wood and kitchen fittings across the yard and into the house.

But he had no choice.

"Yeah, go ahead," he said. "Thanks for bringing everything out here, Kyle, I appreciate it."

"No worries," said Kyle, and hung up.

It took Paul another twenty minutes to get to the house. He pulled onto the hard earth of the fenced-in front yard and looked around. He got out of the car, walked to the back of the house, then around to the front again. Then he pulled out his phone.

"Hey man, wh...at's up?"

He had lost most of his signal; Kyle's voice was crackling and fuzzy.

"Uh... Kyle? Where did you leave the stuff?"

"Just in the fro...nt yard. Hey, sorry about the fe...nce, we'll fix it when we're back up the...re, ...kay?"

Paul turned and looked at the fence. He couldn't see anything. It was not in great condition, but it appeared to be the same as when he had last seen it.

"Did you say the fence?"

"Wh...at? I can't hear you."

"What's wrong with the fence?"

"Yeah, we'll f...ix it, don't worry," said Kyle. "Nice place, by the way. You didn't te...ll me there were fruit trees."

Paul lowered the phone from his ear for a moment.

Oh, no. No, no, no...

"Kyle," he said, raising the phone once more, "how did you find the place? Did you use the directions I gave you?"

"Naw, m...an, what century are you from? We u...sed the GPS."

Paul hung up and ran for his car.

When he arrived at the farm, the woman was standing out front, staring down at a large pile of planks and two sinks, complete with fittings. The mess took up about half the small yard.

He leaped from his truck and into apology mode once more, trying to explain what had happened, though he stopped in his tracks when he saw the fence. Two of the posts had been flattened, and the sections around it had been dragged down as well, sagging low over the ground.

"And they – they said they did that," he said, pointing. "When I called them, they mentioned it – "

"I'd guessed as much," said the woman.

"They were in a hurry."

"That seems to be a common problem."

"Yeah, uh..." Even through the heat of the sun, Paul felt his face flushing. He felt a desperate need to explain himself to this woman who stood looking at him so calmly. "It was the GPS, it... um, do you know how a GPS works?"

The woman raised an eyebrow.

"Do *you*?" she asked.

Paul hesitated. Then he saw the corner of her mouth twitch, and noticed that her eyes were twinkling. And he could not help but break into a smile, albeit a shamefaced one, ducking his head and rubbing the back of his neck.

"Fair enough," he said. He turned and looked over the mess that had been left. "I'll clear this out of the way."

"I don't think it's going to fit in there," said the woman, nodding at his truck.

"I'll have to make a few trips, but it'll be fine," he said, trying to sound as though it would be, even as he realized that he was in for an afternoon of back-breaking work. "And I'll fix your fence, of course," he added.

The woman nodded. "Thank you, Mr...?"

"Jameson, Paul Jameson," said Paul.

He stopped himself from sticking his hand out to shake, thinking that the woman would probably have rules about touching. She simply nodded at him.

"Emma Miller," she said.

"Nice to meet you, Emma Miller," said Paul, and he turned to the pile next to them, bracing himself for the work ahead.

Three hours later, Paul had only just reached the half way point. He had sweated all the way through his shirt and his back and arms were aching. He had made several trips to and from Oak Crest, driving carefully so as not to drop any of the planks that he had been forced to lash into place across the back of his truck, as they would not fit inside.

But he had not allowed himself to stop, and was back once more to pick up the next load. He had just parked his truck in place, backing it up carefully, when the door to the house opened and the little girl came out. She came up to meet Paul as he got out of the car, and handed him what she was carrying – a tall glass of iced water.

"*Mamme* thought you'd be thirsty," she said.

Paul took the glass, wet with condensation, and downed it in a matter of seconds. It was, he decided, the best drink he had had in his entire life.

"You were thirsty," said the girl, taking the glass back. "Do you want another one?"

"Thanks," said Paul, his breath a little short. "Oh, and – Beth, was it?"

The girl stopped.

"Thanks again for helping me down from the tree." he smiled at her.

She grinned back, showing off an endearingly large gap between her front teeth. "Sure," she said.

Paul continued with his work until Beth reappeared with the water; he sipped this glass a little slower, leaning back against the searing side of the truck.

Beth remained with him as he drank, and began asking questions about what he was doing, and why he needed all the planks.

Paul explained about his cabinet and furniture company, and how he was fixing up his uncle's house to sell, and that he had decided to do the work himself. He did not tell her that it was his shame over his inadvertent break-in that had caused him to do some soul-searching and figure out why he felt the need to be in such a rush. He had decided that doing the work himself would be something his uncle would have approved of, too.

Beth was nodding seriously. "My *mamme* says the best job is the one you do yourself."

"She's very right," said Paul, returning the glass once more. "I haven't done any real work like this since I started running the company. I think this serves me right for going soft."

Beth laughed, and headed back to the house. As Paul looked at her retreating figure, he saw that Emma was standing in the doorway. He supposed she had been keeping an eye on her daughter. Though she could not have been too worried, as she had remained at a distance; she smiled a little as they made eye contact.

"Thank you for the water," he called over.

"Sure," she called back. "Don't worry, I'm sure it won't make you soft."

Paul chuckled as he returned to his work.

By the time the sun had dipped to just above the horizon, washing everything in yellows and oranges, Paul was down to his last load. The second part of the work had gone much quicker than the first, as Beth had come out to speak with him every time he came back to pick up a new load, bringing him a glass of water or piece of fruit every once in a while.

This time, it was Emma who stood in the shade of the porch, watching his approach. Paul nodded to her as he stepped from the truck, and she walked forward.

"Looks like you're about done," she said.

"Just about," he agreed. "I can come back tomorrow to see to the fence."

"No rush," said Emma. "We've no animals to keep in, these days."

"No, I guess…" Paul glanced around at the farm. "Did you used to? I mean, your husband, how long, if you don't mind me asking – "

He was not doing a good job of phrasing the question, and stopped, feeling awkward; Emma, however, smiled at him, though her eyes were sad.

"Two years," she said. "I had to give up the farm, though I kept the house. It's just me and Beth now."

Paul nodded. "I'm sorry." He looked around again. "May I ask – if it's not impolite – how you support yourself here?"

"We grow our own vegetables," said Emma. "And extra, to sell. The fruit also does well at the farmers' markets – but it's mainly the rosemary."

"Rosemary?"

"Can't you smell it?" asked Emma.

Paul took in a deep breath, catching anew the scent that had risen in thickness as the day had gone on. He had certainly noticed it, though this was the first time he was able to identify it.

"Of course," he said. "Yes, I was wondering."

"We've a big patch of it out back, nearly a half-acre."

"And you sell it?"

"Yes. Fresh, dried, in bottles of oil or vinegar… you name it." Emma smiled.

"It really smells amazing," said Paul, drinking in the scent, and wondering why he had waited so long to ask what it was.

"I don't notice it quite so much any more," said Emma. "I'm around it all the time. But I miss it when I go somewhere else."

Paul nodded. "It's nice you have a smell you can identify as home," he said.

Emma nodded. She hesitated, then asked, "Do you have anything like that?"

Paul thought for a moment. Then he smiled. "Sawdust," he said.

"Sawdust?"

"Yeah. It's got a kind of sweet smell. My uncle and I used to build things when he'd visit."

"Is this the same uncle that left you the house?"

"Yeah." Paul felt his face go soft as he remembered the times they had spent together. "We even built a boat, one time."

"You built a boat?" Emma raised her eyebrows and smiled, her eyes crinkling mischievously. "Did it float?"

"Sure did," said Paul grinning. "I mean, it was way too round, and we couldn't get the mast to balance, but it floated. We took it fishing a couple of times."

They spoke for a few more minutes, Emma telling Paul about how she had gone fishing when she was a little girl, and Paul telling Emma about how his father and brothers had always refused to go with him, but that his uncle had always agreed. He felt a little surprised as he spoke, that he was sharing something so personal with a stranger. But time seemed to have slowed, making every minute count for an hour, and he could not help feeling comfortable with the small woman in her strange bonnet.

"The first time I met my husband was down by that stream," Emma was saying, pointing to the brook across the road from the house. "We were both little – Beth's age – "

Then she hesitated for a moment, her hand still outstretched, glancing at Paul as though she, too, were surprised that she could be speaking of such things with a stranger.

They were interrupted by the appearance of Beth, who came to confess to dropping an oil bottle.

"I'm sorry, *mamme.*"

"It's all right, *liebchen,* we'll scrub it up with salt," said Emma. "We've plenty more."

"Is this the rosemary oil?" asked Paul.

"Essential oil," said Emma, "to sell at a gift shop in Harperville."

"It's good for you. It's got anti-tabacco properties," Beth informed Paul.

Paul blinked at her for a second. "...Anti-bacterial?" he suggested politely.

"That's what I meant," Beth said gravely.

"I know," he said, just as gravely. From the corner of his eye, he saw Emma covering a smile.

Having driven all the way home to the city that evening, Paul then made the ninety minute drive back out the following day, in order to fix the fence. Emma looked surprised to see him, but smiled nonetheless. Beth was ecstatic, and seemed to have come up with a hundred new questions to ask him during the night. Paul talked with her as he worked, and then with Emma, when she came out to see how everything was going.

He discovered that one of the fence posts had been cracked; he made a support for it, and promised to replace it. Emma told him not to rush, but the next weekend he was back, having used his company's workshop after hours to make a post to exactly the right specifications. He would not want to leave Emma without a fence, after all, and what were a couple more drives?

And then, the week after that, he thought of a few things that he really should see to at Oak Crest, and drove up again, and just happened to pass Emma and Beth on the road, and it would have been rude not to stop and say hello. And Emma happened to mention that she needed muslin fabric to make sachets for her dried rosemary, and Paul remembered that there was a fabric store down the street from his office.

When he returned with the fabric the next weekend, and mentioned that he would be returning again the next week, and to let him know if there was anything else he could bring, Emma commented that he must have found a lot to do at his house. He nodded, blushing only a little.

It was true, in the end. Talking to Emma about the building he had used to do with Ethan, and feeling the old ache in his muscles when he had woken up the day after hauling the wood from her yard, Paul had been flooded with memories of when he had spent his days not making phone calls and tallying costs, but working with his hands, making things that he could be proud of.

He had called the realtor and told him that he would not only be fitting the kitchen himself, but seeing to the rest of the repairs as well, taking his time and working by hand. The realtor had not been pleased at the delay, as he had already had some interest, but the idea of a hand-finished house had appealed to him. He had started using words like "authentic" and "rustic" with a far-off look in his eyes, which Paul could have sworn reflected dollar signs.

He had ignored all of this, and worked solidly on the farmhouse, every weekend and even any evenings he could spare.

And every time he went back to the city, he found himself noticing the smell. The fumes, the trash, the smoke. It followed him everywhere, and he found himself stopping work in the middle of the day to think wistfully of pear trees and long dirt roads leading to quiet places.

After one weekend, when he had driven over with some earthenware plant pots he had found in the Oak Crest garden that he did not have a use for and thought Emma might – he did not want them to go to waste, after all – Emma gave him some rosemary to hang from the mirror of his car.

That was the evening, as Paul sat making some repairs to her front steps that he had noticed needed doing, that Emma opened up about her husband. How close they had been, and how she had struggled after his death, which had come so suddenly in the form of unexpected heart failure.

"He was my best friend," Emma said, again with that slightly surprised expression, as though she had not been expecting to hear the words she spoke.

And Paul had told her of how he had struggled as the third of five sons, always awkward and out of place, and how he had only ever felt like himself when he got to spend time with his uncle.

"But then I started work, and he moved away up here," he said. "I missed him, but I never did anything about it. I still miss him."

Then Emma gave him the rosemary. "It's also used for remembering," she said.

He spent his commutes thinking of jokes he might tell Beth, and of ways to draw out one of Emma's smiles.

By the time Paul had finished his work on the house, the fields he drove past every weekend – with the windows rolled all the way down to chase out the city smell – had been burnished bright gold, and he could see some of the trees had begun to pick up a russet tinge. The heat had not yet abated, however, and the heat carried the scent of rosemary for several hundred yards in every direction from Emma's house. Paul could smell it as he drove past on his way to Oak Crest one Friday afternoon, having put in extra hours at work that week so he could leave early. He was hoping to catch a glimpse of Emma or Beth, and have a reason to stop, but he did not see them, and he had not brought them anything.

He had done a good deal of research into Amish ways of life since meeting the pair of them, as well as several others round about the community who had known his uncle. He knew that it would be inappropriate to simply knock on the door and visit; he had never even been inside their house. He had found himself wishing... well. Wishing.

As he drove up to Oak Crest, he found himself looking forward to the weekend. He had brought up his sleeping bag to stay on the floor, though he would need to go to pick up some take out this evening. The kitchen had yet to be furnished with appliances, and he would not be able to cook. As he got out of the car and looked around, Paul wondered what it would be like to live here; actually live here, not just for holidays. To have quiet every day, and not to have to rush for anything. To not have a phone, or a car. To spend your days on things you actually cared about.

He had been thinking about that a lot recently. But what could he do about it?

Paul's phone chimed.

It was a message from the realtor. There was a couple who were interested – they had seen his latest photos of the new kitchen and bathroom and been particularly impressed. But they wanted an updated photo of the front of the house – Paul had made some improvements to the veranda and had fixed the gutters and roof, and they wanted to see what he had done.

The realtor had included the price they might be offering, which was an absolutely staggering amount, and had finished the message with a series of exclamation points and an insistence that Paul not wait. *Time of the essence!!!* He had added.

Paul sighed deeply, and walked as far back as he needed to in order to get a snap of the front of the house. The vines around the porch had begun to stain themselves wine-red, glowing against the white front of the recently painted clapboards. He wished he could stay and watch them turn fully. How long would that take?

Sorry I can't sell the house right now, Paul imagined messaging his realtor, as he pressed "send." *I'm waiting for the leaves to change. Can we try again in a few months?*

The photo showed a loading symbol. Another message appeared.

They're waiting for the pics now, wrote the realtor, *about to leave office.*

Paul walked around to the side of the house, intending to head for the wall where he had found signal before. He stopped for a moment, looking at the wilderness of the back garden, thinking of what he could do with it if he had time. He could plant a vegetable garden in there, the soil was good and there was plenty of space. He could build a workshop in the space at the side of the house.

He wondered what the couple who wanted to buy the house would do with the garden. Put in a lawn, he guessed, and cut it far too often, most likely. They'd probably tear out the kitchen he had built if they ever wanted to resell.

He felt his phone buzz again, and ignored it.

He heard a voice behind him.

"Paul!"

"Hi there," Paul said, feeling his face light up with a smile as he saw Beth, with Emma in tow.

He had not realized how much he had been missing them; he looked at Emma's cool, friendly face, and Beth's excited smile, and felt his chest ache as though with recognition of something important and far away.

"We missed you!" said Beth, bounding up.

Paul grinned at her, though he felt an urge to look at Emma and determine whether she was invested in Beth's use of the word *we*.

"Someone came with this," said Emma, holding up a box she was carrying. "You weren't home and they said they had to leave it with a neighbor, I guess we're the closest."

"Oh, thanks," said Paul, taking the package. "It's probably the faucet I ordered for the pantry."

"Are we interrupting something?" asked Emma, nodding at the phone in Paul's hand."

Paul glanced down at the thing. "Oh – well, I was just sending a message."

"I'm surprised you have reception out here."

"I have to go into the garden to send it."

"I can take it," offered Beth. She looked so eager that Paul handed the phone over without a second thought.

Beth rushed off, and Paul called after her to be careful not to trip. "It's a jungle in there," he warned.

Then he stopped as a thought hit him.

"Oh – is it okay that she's doing that?" he asked Emma worriedly. "Sorry, I didn't – "

"It's fine," Emma assured him. "She knows not to try and use it without asking permission."

"Okay," said Paul, as they began to walk after Beth. "I kind of wish I had to ask permission to use it," he confided.

"Really."

"Yeah. *Modern inconveniences*, my uncle always called them."

Emma laughed. "You sound as though you might be more suited to a Plain life," she said – and looked away quickly, her mouth snapping shut.

Paul felt an involuntary intake of breath. He had not imagined that, had he?

Had he?

And if that had been what he thought, then this might be it. His only chance to speak.

"I've... well, I have been thinking about it," he said, slowly and deliberately.

He wanted to tell Emma about all the research he had done, and inquiries, pretending to himself at the time that it had just been for the sake of interest, realizing now why he had really done it. But he did not want to start rambling.

He watched Emma's face, but she seemed to be very carefully looking ahead of her, and simply nodded.

"What do you think?" he pressed.

"Well," said Emma, with forced briskness, waving to Beth, who was sitting on the dividing wall and watching a butterfly as it darted among the flowers. "I think that's a very important decision, and one you should bring before God."

Paul nodded. "I think... I think that God might have brought it before me," he said quietly.

Emma paused. "I suppose He did send you a house."

Paul stopped walking. Emma stopped too, a step ahead of him, and slowly turned back.

Paul shook his head. "He sent me to you," he said.

Emma looked up at him. All the breath seemed to rush out of her.

"He did, didn't He?" she said, her voice catching in her throat. "He sent you to me. And to Beth."

"And to Beth," said Paul, looking over at the little girl, adventuring in the greenery of the garden which would, soon enough, be hers to play in by right. He imagined, allowed himself to imagine, just for a moment, what it might be like to call her his own. And he felt as though his heart might burst from his chest. "I've been so grateful for the time we've spent together."

"As have I." Emma's eyes were damp. "The way I've felt these past few months, I thought – I kept thinking – even if I couldn't – if you were going to leave, and that was it, I was still so grateful."

Paul stared at her.

"Grateful?" he asked, incredulous. "For me? You grateful for me, are you kidding? The crazy English guy who tried to break into your house?"

"I think that might have been God's way of getting my attention," Emma said, trying to smile, her voice thick. "We laughed about it, after you'd gone, Beth and I, and she said that she couldn't remember the last time I had laughed. She said she hoped you'd come back. And you did."

Paul wished he had a handkerchief to offer her, or even a paper tissue. He felt, suddenly, an urge to move – but hesitated. He knew that he would not be able to be really affectionate with Emma; the rules seemed to be different in different places, but he did not want to make any assumptions. He would have to be willing to wait until they were married, and that would take a while if he went about it the right way. Which he would – he would take his time, and do it right. No rushing, not any more.

But for now, he reached out toward a tear that had dripped onto Emma's cheek, swimming amongst her freckles. With the utmost care, he wiped it away.

She closed her eyes as he did so, inhaling deeply. When she opened them again, she smiled.

"You smell like sawdust," she said.

A MENDING AMISH HEART

LUCY DAWSON

The train screeched to a halt and Elaine Sheldon had to brace herself for the onslaught of people trying to squeeze past out. Holding tightly around the handrail, she winced when a rushing man bumped his laptop bag against her hips, and she took a few steps back with the impact.

The man did not stop to apologize and Elaine only heaved a sigh and fixed her stance as the train resumed moving.

It was supposed to be a twenty-minute walk from the station to her home, but tonight, it did not feel like it. Her steps were slow and her shoulders were drooped. The streetlights refused to turn on properly and it flickered repeatedly as she passed by. Elaine sighed at the dreary atmosphere.

Just a week ago, these walks home passed by with a spring in her step, looking forward to the person who was waiting for her to be back, the person she had been going home to for the past six months, the man who welcomed her with a warm hug and a big smile after a tiring day at work—until the other day.

Someone new had moved in next door and as she walked by she saw boxes stacked in front of the front of the door. The sound of a man's groans can be heard as she came closer.

She battled with herself if she should help or not. As the next-door neighbor, she knew she should, as a sign of welcome for the new occupant, but she also knew that the feeling in her chest is heavier than those boxes. She scoffed at her dramatics but looked down at herself. Her arms were already crying in protest with her own bag and those boxes looked nowhere near light so she forgot being thoughtful for once and unlocked her door. She was about to go inside when a man's voice startled her.

"Hi. Do you live next door?" The man beamed at her but the smile didn't reach his eyes.

Elaine smiled back, a closed-lip one. "And you must be my new neighbor," she offered her hand which the man accepted. "Elaine."

"Ivan. It's nice to meet you," he let go of her hand and gestured at the boxes. "I'll be done in a minute. You don't have to worry about the noises." He smiled again but Elaine can only see a grimace.

"Don't worry, take your time. I would have helped you but—"

Ivan waved his hand no. "No need. You must be tired from work," he observed, noticing the formal attire and the bag hanging on her shoulders. "Go on ahead. Have a good night."

"You too," she returned in a clip tone and sent a brief smile again before going inside. The bang of the door echoed throughout the dark empty unit, reminding Elaine that she had no company anymore, that she had to spend the night alone in her empty house.

A tear escaped down her cheeks, which ended with bouts of sobbing for the third consecutive night.

—-

There are things in life that once you get a taste of, you'd never want to let go. And for Elaine, that was her relationship with Christian.

They started dating a little over a year ago, when they met at a Sunday event singing. The spent the entire evening chatting away. A week later, they found themselves agreeing to date exclusively.

Elaine did not have high hopes with her relationship at the start. Christian seemed to be the happy-go-lucky type of guy who always acted on a whim instead of having plans. She wasn't in too deep yet, so she didn't mind it at all.

But as the months go by and their relationship turned for the better, people around them started to notice—that Christian was changing for the good and it was mainly because of his relationship with Elaine. It flattered the female, she won't deny it. Knowing that she may be one of the reasons why Christian was trying to find a stable job, having the courage to pursue his passion in painting. He would always go off on his own and paint flat stones, an odd pursuit for an Amish man. He became so good at it that a local art dealer encouraged him to go to art school. He began making plans for his future and this pleased Elaine.

All along, Elaine was expecting that she was included in the plan. It only dawned on her that she was never part of the picture when one day she saw Christian arrive at her steps with a large bag filled with all of his belongings.

At first, she thought he was going for a vacation. She could've accepted it, a six-month out of the country trips to take images of the wonders of nature. What she didn't understand was why he had to break up with her.

They could've made it worked, Elaine believed so. She trusted herself to stay faithful and she put the same amount of trust on Christian. It just so happened that her ex-boyfriend did not believe in long distance relationships. It even hurt more when he said that he's not even sure if he's even coming back.

"I want to see what else is out there," he said. "I've been accepted into art school and this could be the beginning of a completely new life."

Intellectually, Elaine understood. But all so could do was cry. She begged him to at least try and make them work but he was already decided.

And that was it. The end of a year-long courtship in just a snap.

—

The minister was going through the sermon part and Elaine pinched her forearm to stay focused. They had to work overtime last night and she barely had a wink of sleep before she raced to be on time to the church.

Attending the church was a weekly thing for Elaine. Christian never accompanied her no matter how much she forced him to and now, she became secretly grateful because at the least, she has this one activity she was used to doing alone.

The minister's voice resounded against the walls and she snapped back into attention.

"The Lord knows what is best for each of His children," the minister intoned.

I don't know about that, Elaine thought. *Christian was what was best for me and now he's gone. I feel like I'm in a dark tunnel without any light to guide me out. If you really know what's best, Lord, then show me. Please.*

Then someone, a man perhaps judging by the black slacks and the scent, sat beside her. She almost rolled her eyes for the man's tardiness but bit her lips when she realized that she was no better for daydreaming instead of listening.

The minister droned on and and her eyelids grew heavier and heavier.

By the time she woke up, people were standing up and were walking towards the exit. Elaine jolted in her seat, lifting her head from a sturdy shoulder she was leaning on, cheeks crimsoning due to the embarrassment.

She looked to her right and her eyes widened while the color of her cheeks got redder. "Ivan," she muttered. Of all people to fall asleep on while a mass was ongoing, it had to be her new next-door neighbor.

Ivan chuckled and raised his hand to his lip, which confused Elaine. When it dawned on her, she turned around and wiped the bit of drool that escaped her lips.

Clearing her throat and checking discreetly if there was still drool left, she turned back again to an amused Ivan. At least now, the smile reached his eyes unlike the first time she saw him.

"I'm sorry for falling asleep on you," she pursed her lips. An old lady passing by gave her a stink eye and she refused to shrink on her seat in shame.

Her neighbor saw the gesture and he chuckled. "It's okay. You went home late didn't you?"

"How did you know?"

Ivan looked more amused now. "I heard your door slam. It wasn't exactly hard to hear when it's the dead hour of the morning."

Elaine nodded, laughing at herself for thinking of anomalous things such as Ivan being a stalker or a creep. It crossed her mind that it was still strange for him to be awake at such an hour but then that would mean it was also strange for her to have just come home so she didn't bring it up.

"Oh!" She unconsciously glanced over his shoulder and found a tiny, wet mark. Scrambling for tissues, she pulled a handful and wiped at his clothes furiously. "I am so sorry," she apologized repeatedly until Ivan had to hold her hand to stop her.

"It's spit. No big deal. No one's gonna die," he smiled once again. Elaine thought he should smile more often. It brightens up his face. Meanwhile, her face was on fire.

"Can I treat you for coffee then? As sorry and welcome?"

"I'd love to but I have somewhere to be. Maybe next time," he said noncommittally.

"Next time then." She apologized again before racing back home.

***

Elaine dragged her feet to the sofa and flopped down unceremoniously with her legs hanging on an arm. Tears cascaded down her temples, which progressed into sobs. Her chest felt tight and her breath was constricted.

Earlier, she prayed to God to give her Christian back. She wished that Christian would change his mind and call her, or at least send her a message, saying he made a big mistake and that he wanted her back.

She was praying but still felt the pain of loss. She asked God why did this have to happen to her, why she had to feel such pain, why she had to feel hopeful for her future for once, only for it to crumble right in front of her.

It was so unfair. She gave it her all but all she got was nothing.

—-

It had been a month since the breakup and Elaine was faring better. She hadn't cried herself to sleep for two weeks now and she even had the energy to go out for a walk. It wasn't much but it was a start. She still thought of Christian from time to time but the pangs of loss were getting less painful. In a way she didn't know how, she began to heal.

It was a Sunday and she was on her way to the church. A friend, Leslie, welcomed her with a bright smile.

"You're looking great, dear," she said.

"How have you been, Leslie? I haven't seen you here lately?"

Leslie beamed at her in delight. "I took a trip. To France! Oh, we have to get some coffee later. I have lots of stories to tell you," she narrated giddily, the smile never wavering off her face.

"That's great," Elaine said. She didn't long to visit far away places like some of her other Amish friends but she enjoyed hearing the stories.

"How's Christian? Bet he's at home sleeping?" Leslie chuckled and Elaine's eyes twitched. She swallowed a lump in her throat and an awkward silence passed before her friend realized that something was wrong.

"Hey, what's wrong?"

Elaine cleared her throat and forced a smile. "W-we broke up," she cursed at herself for stuttering. It felt more real every time she had to say it outloud and it doubled the sharp pain that coursed through her.

Leslie looked shocked beyond belief at the news and caressed Elaine's arm. "I'm so sorry!"

"It's okay. It's been a month."

She wiped the tears that escaped despite her resistance. "I'm all right," she forced out a smile. Her friend looked at her worriedly but let it go for now. "All right, let's have lunch together okay?" Leslie asked, to which Elaine said yes. It had been a while since she had a meal with another person aside from her co-workers and she welcomed the thought now more than ever.

The service lasted for a little over an hour after which the two young women went to the Farmer's Market for lunch.

"I'm *hungerich*," Leslie announced to the world. "And I'm just dying for some *pannekuche*. Some *pannekuche* or maybe some shoofly pie."

"Sounds good to me."

Elaine was grateful for the distraction but she could not help but glance at a table for two at a furthest corner. She remembered sunny days sitting with Christian, eating the different treats, talking and laughing.

***

Elaine was preparing to bake a pie when a call came. Not expecting anybody, she looked at her phone quizzically, which registered Leslie's name. Leslie rarely contacted her through the phone as even though Amish teenagers now had cell phones, not many of her friends actually used the device.

Surprised, she accepted the call and had to brace herself for a joyful Leslie who almost screeched a 'hello.'

"Hey, what's up?" Elaine reclined back on her seat and shut her eyes. She could hear her stomach grumbling only to remember that she didn't eat anything for lunch.

"I know this might be too soon, but it's been two months and it's not too soon right?" She said rapidly and Elaine had to sit up straight again and focus on her words to keep up.

"What exactly might be too soon?"

Leslie paused dramatically. Elaine could almost hear her excitement through the receiver.

"Dating."

"Dating?" Elaine repeated dumbly.

"Yeah, dating. I figure it's about time you meet new people. What do you think?" Elaine processed everything before saying an alarmed 'what' as a reaction.

She sighed before continuing. "Leslie, I know you have the best intentions in mind. But if you still didn't know, I barely have time to meet new people."

"But you have the time," Leslie insisted. "Every other Sunday you're at church."

"I do. But that's for church and some me time. I don't feel like going to a party or anything after a service."

"Exactly. For church. And forget the me time, you have more than enough of that," Leslie paused and apologized for the insensitive remark, which Elaine only waved away. Leslie was just telling the truth.

"What I actually wanted to say is that I know this guy, from the church we go to, who you might be interested to meet," Leslie drawled on. It took a minute before it registered what she was suggesting.

"Are you setting me up on a blind date?" She asked incredulously.

"Uh, yes," her friend admitted sheepishly.

Elaine rubbed a thumb on a temple. "Do I have a say on this?"

"Not really. I already set up the time and date."

"Leslie—!"

"I had to! I know you're gonna say no!"

"Whatever. Just text me the details. I have work to do," Elaine grumbled. She heard a faint 'I love you' before she hung up the phone and she felt a little bad for not saying it back to her dear friend.

—-

That night, Elaine turned and tossed on her bed. She couldn't stop thinking about the blind date and she had bombarded herself with too much questions that only left her more confused and doubtful.

Is it too soon? What if Christian knows about it? What if the guy isn't what she's expecting him to be? But then, what exactly are her expectations?

The fact that he goes to her church is a good point, but the thought that she saw it as a good point gnawed at her guilt. It might be ridiculous but she felt guilty for indirectly saying yes to the blind date. It had been two months but thinking of a possibility of a relationship with anyone other than Christian brought a bad taste to her mouth.

—-

Elaine pushed the glass door open before a waitress assisted her to her seat. A man was already seated at the table, but she could not see his face yet.

A gasp escaped her lips when the waitress stopped and gestured at their table, making the man look up.

"Elaine?" Ivan said, sounding shell-shocked himself.

"You're Leslie's friend?" Elaine asked for good measure. She had not seen her neighbor for weeks now. The last time, they only exchanged brief hellos when they happened to meet while taking out trash.

Ivan stood up and helped her pull her seat back, before returning to his own side.

"And you are Leslie's friend," Ivan jokingly deadpanned. Elaine took her seat and began to chuckle. Ivan, amused by the situation, also began to laugh.

"I guess we'll be having a date today?" He asked with a smile on his face. Elaine hummed in affirmation while smiling from ear to ear.

"How did you meet Leslie?" Elaine asked once their food was served.

"We had a mutual friend. A guy named Ethan. He was an old friend and he was the one who suggested this place for me to move to," Ivan explained before taking a bite of the grilled chicken.

Elaine took a sip of water before responding. "Why did you move? Was it for your job?"

The question froze Ivan for a second before he relaxed. Elaine bit her tongue for the question which obviously hit a nerve.

"You don't have to answer it if you don't want to."

"Sorry," he offered a timid smile.

"It's okay," she smiled before diverting the conversation to a different topic.

It turned out that they have a lot of similar interests than they could have expected. They both loved fishing, volleyball and horseback riding.

Hours later, they found themselves laughing comfortably around each other while they walked home. They stopped when they reached Elaine's door and Ivan kept a good distance, to which Elaine was grateful for.

"I really had a lot of fun," Ivan smiled.

"Me too. I think it's been ages since I've laughed that much," Elaine gushed.

He put his hands in his pant's back pockets and Elaine mentally chuckled.

"We should do this again some other time?" It was more of a question rather than a statement.

Elaine let out a deep breath she didn't know she had been holding and nodded. "Sure."

***

She threw the frame inside the black plastic bag and flinched at the sound of breaking glass. Next were the love letters that he had written her, painstaking essays of everlasting love that he would never commit to.

It was a day after her blind date and last night, she had the urge to throw away everything that reminded her of Christian. It had been months but she still kept some of their photographs of them being together.

This move did not mean anything but a sign of her trying to move on. She had been meaning to do it for weeks but the date with Ivan was the last push she needed to start working on it. She sniffed and sobbed for the first few minutes but it got better as she tore a few of the love letters to shreds.

Soon she had a garbage bag filled with pictures, letters, dried flowers, candy and chocolate wrappers, and almost every single thing that Christian gave her during their relationship, including the bracelet that he gifted to her last Christmas. It took a lot of emotional effort but afterwards, she felt lighter, as if an invisible baggage was thrown away.

The door next to her opened just as she was pulling the plastic bag outside to throw it in the bin. Ivan looked as surprised as she was.

"Don't mind me," he said. "Just going for a walk."

Elaine stopped for a second to think before taking a leap of faith. "Mind if I join you?"

—

The night was a bit chilly but fortunately, there was minimal wind.

They walked through the streets, enjoying the fact that they were the only ones around.

She looked at him curiously. "How long have you been going for walks at night?" She asked as Ivan slowed his walking pace a bit.

"Since the first week I moved," he answered. "It was a bit lonely staying indoors."

Elaine stopped in her tracks, causing Ivan to stop too.

"I am so sorry for being a very unwelcoming neighbor. I should have made you something and came over to check on you."

Ivan rested a hand on her head and ruffled her hair. Elaine felt like pulling away but didn't, surprised at how large his hand felt. "No need to feel sorry. I know it wasn't your best day then," he continued walking and she followed automatically.

She gulped as she remembered that day. It was definitely one of her most miserable days. "Yeah. My boyfriend just broke up with me a few days before that," she chuckled dryly. This time, it was Ivan who stopped first.

"I am so sorry to hear that."

She pursed her lips in thought. "It's okay. I've been doing great. It wasn't an excuse to not welcome you," she patted his shoulder, signaling him to continue moving.

It was silent for a few minutes before Ivan spoke up again.

"I just got divorced a few months ago."

Elaine screeched to a halt. "What?" Her eyes widened at her rude reaction. "I mean, when?"

"A few weeks before I moved," Ivan looked down. "My ex-wife and I just got divorced and I realized I can't stay at our home for long so I sold it, and moved here," he gestured at the surroundings. "And I think I made a great decision."

"I am sorry to hear that," Elaine said. "Your divorce, I mean."

"I guess we're both sorry to hear about each other's heartbreaks?"

***

They continued to contact each other throughout the week. Elaine frequently opted to work until late at the baker so they couldn't really meet much. Leslie called once to check on how the date went and squealed when Elaine responded with a simple 'Thank you' and then Leslie shouted 'I knew it, I knew it' repeatedly until it burned Elaine's ears.

The following Sunday, Elaine and Ivan agreed to go to the church together, causing Leslie to get excited upon seeing them.

She looked at them knowingly and winked at Elaine, who blushed at her friend's action. Ivan chuckled at the sight but pretended that he did not see it.

During the mass, Elaine prayed and asked for guidance, if what she was doing was right or if it was too soon to consider liking a different man. When she opened her eyes and looked at Ivan's direction, she found him to be staring back at her.

She glanced away and fought down the blush that crept on her cheeks.

—

It was a Wednesday night and usually, Elaine would still be at work, doing things that were not really urgent.

When she got home, it was way too early for bedtime and she found herself thinking of the man living in the house beside hers. Curiously, she opened her window and listened for any noises in his home.

Then a knock came at her door. She opened up and was welcomed by the sight of Ivan.

"Do you want to go for a walk?"

**

A chilly air greeted them as they walked down the winding lane. They found themselves walking close to each other, shoulders almost bumping. Elaine looked at her side and it was only a few inches away from Ivan's. Unconsciously, she continued to stare until he looked back.

"Like what you see?" he grinned mischievously, earning a smack on his chest.

"Your scar," she started, pertaining to a small scar at the left corner of his lips.

"Ah, they're battle scars," he jested. Her forehead scrunched at the vague answer.

"I had a bit of a scuffle last year. I saw my then wife with another man and I confronted them right on the spot. And the rest is history," he smiled but the bitterness was pronounced.

They walked another block before Ivan put his arm around her. It was a bold move and she held her breath for a moment. She gave in to his touch, leaning her head on his shoulder and let the tension seep out of her body.

"I only have one question," she said after a while.

"What is it?" he closed his eyes, hoping that he could answer it whatever the question was.

"He got it worse right? I mean, you managed to hit his face at least twice? With bruises?"

Ivan burst out laughing. "Yes, yes, I did. I kicked him in the stomach, too. It was pretty satisfying," he answered, still chuckling at the unexpected question.

"Good."

They walked the rest of the way, his arm around her shoulders.

***

Elaine placed her cake into the oven when the owner of the bakery stepped into the kitchen.

"I just got a call back from the Petersons," he said.

Elaine waited with bated breath. She had worked hard on the Peterson's cake. A true work of art with a design of a football on top to commemorate their son's sport scholarship.

"And they just raved," he said. "Best tasting cake they ever had. Keep up the good work, young lady, keep up the good work."

"Thank you."

"Whatever you changed, keep it up," he commented, puzzling Elaine.

"What do you mean?"

"I mean, you look happier. Whatever the reason is, continue doing it," he said before turning back to his office.

Elaine could only think of one big change in her life recently. Biting her lips to stop herself from grinning too widely, she smiled at the thought of Ivan.

**

Elaine nearly skipped down the street as she walked home. Feeling confident, she felt like calling on Ivan and asking if he would like to go out to dinner.

But as she neared her home she saw Ivan outside his home, talking on his cell phone.

"I don't care about that," he said in a voice of anger she had never heard him use before. "I'm deleting your number. Please don't call me anymore."

She could only watch as Ivan threw the cell phone to the ground and watched it scatter into different pieces.

"Cell phones," Ivan said. "We should have never let them in the community."

Elaine could only cock her brow at the man. He stared down at the broken device and his chest heaved deeply. Slowly, she walked towards him and reached for his shoulders. He relaxed at the touch and rubbed a hand on his face.

"I'm sorry you have to hear that," he reached for her hand and pulled her closer to him before hugging her waist.

Elaine put her hand on his hair and carded her fingers through the black strands.

"It was my ex-wife," he explained, making Elaine halt her actions for a moment. She only resumed when Ivan nudged her hand with his head. "She was telling me about her wedding in two weeks, and that I'm invited." He laughed bitterly. "She cheated on me and she had the guts to invite me to her wedding."

Elaine, now shaken, fought back tears of empathy. She can feel the hurt in Ivan's voice.

She remained silent, listening to Ivan's breath until he completely relaxed and his breaths evened out.

The silence became deafening until Elaine had the courage to break it. "Do you still love her?"

It was a yes-no question but Ivan didn't respond for the next two seconds, nor even for the next few minutes.

Feeling defeated, Elaine pulled herself from his grasp, ignoring his pleas to come back. She made it back to her own house and slammed the door shut.

Ivan knocked on her door.

"Elaine?" he pleaded. "Elaine, don't do this."

"Please. Stop it. I need some time alone."

The knocks stopped, and a few seconds later, she could hear another door being slammed shut.

—-

Just months ago, it was Christian who was the cause of Elaine's sleepless nights. It was him who was the reason why she cried and continuously asked herself of what's wrong with her and why do people find it so hard to love her. It was him who was the reason why she didn't want to wake up to face another day and tempted her to just laze on her bed, feeling as if all the energy had been sucked out from her.

But now, just a few months later, Ivan had been occupying her mind much more than she expected he would.

He is a good man. He's nice, funny, responsible, smart, and even good-looking—a complete catch if she dared say. When she first saw him, all sweaty and panting from carrying heavy boxes, she just saw him as just another attractive man who happened to be her neighbor and nothing else. Admittedly, she even forgot about him until their embarrassing encounter at the church. That was how it was, but because of one date, it turned into something more.

Elaine found herself genuinely enjoying Ivan's company as they spent more time together. It started from scheduled lunches and walks until they found themselves into a routine of being together every other day, whether it was to just talk or share about their day.

It was a routine that they easily adapted to—they never forced themselves into it nor did they set fixed days and to-do lists whenever they meet. Day by day, Elaine found herself thinking of her ex-boyfriend less, and whenever she did, it was to smile at the memories they shared and never to wallow in the sadness and the gaping hole he made when he left.

As Ivan made her feel light-hearted, carefree and secured, she found herself forgetting about the heartbreaking nights, about the times when she went back to an empty home, and about the thrown away pictures and gifts. With Ivan, she felt that she could try again, that she could, maybe, fall in love again.

But it seemed that Ivan thought otherwise. She could still see how hurt he was when he talked about his ex-wife inviting him to her wedding. She could remember how tightly clenched his fists were and how much he was trembling in anger. It was a sight she never expected to see from the usually composed man.

When she asked that question she wasn't hoping for an absolute no. They were married and she knew that he must have felt so strongly for her to ask for her hand. But at the least, she was expecting something along the lines of 'I'm doing fine' or 'I'm getting over it' and it would have sufficed, for her at least.

If anything, it made her realize how much she was wearing her heart on her sleeve yet again. She wasn't in love with him, not yet at least, but she knew she was on her way. All along, she thought he felt the same, that he was moving forward and trying to forget his past heartbreak, just like her. Elaine thought that a part of him had thought about her in a romantic way, that she might be someone who he can ideally like, but then again, those were just Elaine's assumptions.

The problem with her, as always, were her hopes and baseless assumptions. These always manage to hang her up emotionally—big time. She just never learned.

—

Ivan tried to contact her in the following days but she was resolved on avoiding him for a few days. She was aware that she was being immature but she deemed herself unprepared.

Every day, she recited every line she could say once they managed to talk. She imagined different scenarios and how she would react to them and what she should say. She admitted, most of her thought-of situations were bad. She wasn't too hopeful that they would be returning back to the friendly yet flirty camaraderie they had formed.

Elaine was far from being level-headed. When it came to feelings, she was like an open book. She never tried to hide what she was feeling nor did she ever lie about it. So when one day, while standing on the train, hand clasped tightly on the handrail, she heard Ivan's voice behind her.

"Will you be my girlfriend?"

Turning around and seeing him standing there, she broke down into tears.

Commuters nearby couldn't help but notice the scene.

Among all the scenarios she imagined in her head, this wasn't how it was supposed to be. He wasn't supposed to show out of nowhere and tell her things she has been wishing to hear for weeks in the middle of a crowded train. She tried to stop her tears but the various emotions overwhelmed her.

Ivan had panicked, wiping away her tears furiously with his fingers and then the sleeves of his jacket. He was expecting her to shriek or push him away or to give him the finger, but this wasn't in his imagined reactions.

When the train stopped at the next station, he gently guided Elaine out and continued hushing her. Her cries were now reduced to sobs and Ivan cursed at himself for making her cry.

Once she was calm, she smacked him hard on his chest, before saying a garbled "Yes."

For a while, Ivan was confused why she said that but broke into a large grin when he realized the implication.

Overjoyed, he grabbed her face with both hands and kissed her, right in the middle of the station, with some bystanders looking away from the scene. The kiss was chaste yet sweet. Their lips glided smoothly against each other and for a while, Ivan was tempted to press harder, which was futile when Elaine pushed him.

"But," Elaine sniffed and shushed him with a finger on his lips. "Explain."

"Could we go home first? It's starting to get cold," he took off his own coat and put it around her.

Exiting the train station, he hailed down a cab.

There was a deafening silence throughout the ride home and their way up in the elevator, but Ivan never let go of her hand the whole time.

He led them to his house instead of Elaine's and she was about to protest but he insisted.

Leading her inside, they sat on the sofa. She squirmed in her seat and he gave her some space, rubbing his neck sheepishly.

He reached for her hand and turned his body towards her.

Ivan started with a deep breath before launching to his long narrative. "That night, when you asked me if I still loved her, I was sure that my answer was no," he brought a hand up when he saw that she was about to interrupt him.

He continued once she silently agreed to keep on listening.

"But at the same time, I can't say it. It sounds more real once you say it out loud doesn't it? Am I making any sense?"

"Yes," Elaine nodded. "I felt the same thing about Christian."

"We were a couple since we were eighteen. Most people called us the ideal couple and were just waiting for us to get married. It was as if there was no other way out of it but to build our own family. So I did ask for her hand in marriage and she said yes." Ivan heaved a deep breath, composing his next words in his mind.

"But as soon as we started living together, something felt...weird. A year later, I realized how used we are to being together. We were so used to seeing each other, to doing things together that it only seemed natural that we got married. I realized that maybe, we took marriage for granted, and it was a hurried decision merely out of obligation because of the people's expectations."

"We started to drift away from each other then. In the back of my mind, I knew she was thinking the same thing. When I saw her with another man, it hurt me—not because I still love her but because I was at least expecting that we wouldn't reach that point where we would hide secrets behind each other's backs—especially a lover at that."

"I saw red and then I found myself furious. I was angry at her but more at myself for letting us be trapped in that situation. When we decided on the divorce, it was heartbreaking but it felt like a burden I never knew I had was lifted from me. It felt liberating." He paused, tightening his hold on Elaine's hand. Elaine returned the gesture, egging him to go on.

"I admit. It still hurts. But not because I still love her but more from the fact that I spent so many years thinking I was happy but realized that I wasn't. It was hard coming to terms with that: that I forced myself to think that everything was alright when it wasn't. And then suddenly, she told me the news that she's getting married and practically screaming at me that she's found her happiness. I'm happy for her. We've been together for so long that I can't even bear thinking of hating her. But then I thought of myself and my sorry state of a coward who can't even ask you to be mine and I was enraged because I felt that it was unfair. I thought that I deserve my own happiness too." His voice trembled then and he blinked repeatedly as his eyes began to get misty.

Elaine knelt beside him and pulled his head to her chest, rubbing his back consolingly at the confession.

"I'm sorry if I hurt you. Because all this just came crashing on me and I suddenly couldn't answer. I didn't know where to start. It felt too much." She felt a wetness on her arm and hugged him more tightly. If she could only take a part of the pain he was feeling, she would do it.

"I'm sorry for assuming the worst, and for not giving you a chance to explain." she kissed a spot in his head to reassure him that she was there, and that she wouldn't be leaving anytime soon.

Ivan retreated and pulled her into his lap, resting his forehead against hers. "I'm sorry for giving you the

chance to assume the worst. If anything, I just really want to say how much I like you and how much you make me happy." He gave her a peck and kept his lips there, feeling the smile forming on his lips.

"I'm really glad I met you. I'd do anything I could so you could forget him completely."

Elaine shook her head no in protest. "No, Ivan. We will work together so we could heal completely. This is no you helping me, nor me helping you. This is us helping each other," she said, gazing into his eyes lovingly.

He smiled a smile that reached his eyes, the one that Elaine absolutely adored, before replying. "I love the sound of that."

END

NO PLACE LIKE AN AMISH HOME

STEPHANIE SWIFT

Sarah stood on the sidewalk and stared at the flashing lights above her while people walked right past her as if she were invisible. It felt like her feet were glued to the pavement, and no matter how hard she tried, she couldn't budge. The light bulbs were as big as her hand and there were far too many to count.

"What did you call this?" she asked, pointing upward.

Her childhood friend, Joseph, laughed as he leaned against the brick wall of the Sawmill Movie Theater. His Amish attire was long gone and the bright red t-shirt, jeans, and jacket he wore made him blend in with every other young man who strode past them. It was odd seeing him in such strange clothing, but dressing like the other Dayton residents had always been high on his "to do" list, long before they left home for Rumspringa.

"It's a marquee," he answered. "They use it to let you know what movies are playing inside."

Sarah nodded as she observed the lights twinkling in rapid succession. It was quite fascinating watching them chase each other around and around...although looking at them too long was starting to give her a headache.

"Which one do you want to see?" Joseph asked.

Sarah read the four movie titles on the *marquee* and shrugged her shoulders. "I don't know. I've never been to a theater before. You pick."

Joseph furrowed a brow as he mulled over his choices. "Okay, let's watch The Shining. That sounds interesting."

It honestly didn't matter to Sarah either way because she would be nervous nonetheless. As they made their way inside the front entrance, she felt her heart drum rapidly in her chest. The lobby was dimly lit and full of people from youngsters to the elderly. Joseph walked in front of her and paid their way while she gripped one of the belt loops on his jeans to keep from losing him in the crowd.

They followed the throng of people to a massive corridor with two sets of double doors on each side, and Sarah breathed a little easier when she saw The Shining movie title glowing from a much smaller marquee above one of the doors to their right.

Joseph put his arm protectively around her waist as they opened the doors and walked into yet another dark hallway that seemed to stretch a mile before it opened into an enormous room filled with a huge screen, a tall stairway, and seats that were stacked in rows almost to the ceiling.

"Let's sit closer to the bottom," Joseph suggested.

She wasn't about to argue, since the thought of sitting so high up made her stomach twist in knots. Once they were seated on the second row, Sarah took off her bonnet and stuffed it inside her dress pocket. She envied Joseph being so comfortable in English clothing, but she hadn't managed to take such a big step – at least, not yet.

Several minutes passed before the lights on the walls surrounding them began to dim and the screen came on. The light and noise emanating from it took her by surprise and made her jump, nearly out of her skin. She looked beside her at Joseph, who was clearly enthralled with his wide eyes and slacked jaw.

When the movie started, Sarah's heart began to thrum more rapidly, and she was immediately engrossed in the action. Since their Rumspringa started two weeks prior, she and Joseph had tallied up several new adventures, from visiting an amusement park to dancing the night way at some of the local clubs with a couple of friends from their small Amish community just outside of Dayton, Ohio.

Although their friends had since returned home for good, she and Joseph were still undecided about what path they wanted to take. There were many things about the English way of life that tempted her into staying, but she couldn't deny the fact that a bigger part of her heart longed for home.

Sarah sank back in her seat. The movie was a lot scarier than she expected it would be and probably not the best choice for a first-time moviegoer. When a man wielding an ax filled the screen, she let out a yelp and covered her eyes with her hands, which delighted Joseph to no end and made him nearly choke on his own laughter.

Sarah peeked through her fingers as one of the characters screams filled the air, and she immediately wished she hadn't as the blood and gore made her stomach churn. She leaned over so she could whisper in Joseph's ear. "I'm going to the restroom."

He gave her a quick nod but never took his eyes off the screen. She wasn't even positive he comprehended a word she said, but she was up and walking toward the corridor before he could reply or object. As soon as she stepped through the double doors away from the screams, she breathed a huge sigh of relief.

Sarah went toward the direction of the lobby. She really didn't need to go to the restroom, but she did want to sit down on the long bench she'd spotted in the lobby. The crowd had dispersed since the movie began so hopefully she would be able to enjoy a few minutes of peace and quiet.

Sarah sat down on the bench and removed the bonnet from her pocket so she could put it back on. After wearing one nearly every day of her life since birth, she felt naked without it.

"The Shining?"

A deep, masculine voice filled the air as Sarah turned in the direction it came from. A tall man, who appeared close to her age, stood behind a concession stand to her left. He was leaning over the glass counter, bracing himself on his elbows, and when he smiled at her, Sarah felt a surge of heat rush through her veins.

"Excuse me?" she asked.

He chuckled at her response before gesturing to the bench. "You're pale as a ghost and sitting here in the lobby, so I'm guessing you were watching The Shining."

She touched her cheeks and grinned. "Is it that obvious?"

The stranger walked over to a small refrigerator and pulled out a bottle of soda. "Would you like something to drink? No charge. Maybe it will put some color back in those cheeks."

Sarah joined him at the counter. "Thank you, but you don't have to do that...really."

He set the bottle in front of her and Sarah was immediately taken with his sweet demeanor and good looks. His eyes were the softest brown she'd ever seen – almost golden – and his smile revealed dimples in his cheeks.

"I'm happy too," he replied. "My name is Doug, by the way."

He held out a hand for her to shake, and she felt a lump in her throat as she placed her hand in his, hoping and praying he wouldn't notice how bad she was trembling. "I'm Sarah. It's nice meeting you."

She opened the bottle and took a sip to try and steady her nerves. The lobby was almost vacant, so they were practically alone, which both thrilled and terrified her.

"Please don't take this the wrong way, but I'm surprised to see you here," he remarked.

She saw his eyes drift to her clothing and she realized what he was referring to. It wasn't the first time she'd heard such a comment in the past two weeks. "My friends and I are celebrating Rumspringa. Do you know what that is?"

He leaned forward on the counter again, and when Sarah noticed how close they were, she took a couple of hesitant steps away from him. The temptation to run her fingertips over his dimples was far greater to resist than she anticipated, but if he noticed her trepidation, he didn't mention it.

"We had some Amish neighbors when I was growing up in Pennsylvania, so I've heard about it."

An awkward silence passed between them, but Doug never took his gaze off her, and Sarah did her best to keep from making a fool of herself by taking sips of her soda and fiddling with the label on the bottle.

"So, how long have you lived in Dayton?" she asked.

She cringed because it sounded like such a generic question, but she was running out of ideas to keep the conversation flowing. Doug smiled as he intertwined his fingers together and twiddled his thumbs. He had a mischievous aura about him that was quite adorable, but perhaps it was just the dimples giving him that impression.

"I moved here when I started college last year. I'm a freshman at ITT."

She had no idea what that stood for, but she wasn't about to ask, so she simply nodded like she understood. As far as colleges went, the only one she knew of was Ohio State University, and that was only because she overheard a group of people talking about it at one of the clubs they visited.

"Hey, would you like to grab a cup of coffee with me? There's a café net door, and I get off work in thirty minutes."

Sarah stood up straight and cleared her throat. Was he really asking her on a date? If she had something to compare it with she might know, but she'd never been alone with any other man besides Joseph. He was her best friend though, so that didn't count.

"I would love to, but I need to let my friend know first, and he's still watching the movie."

Doug stood quickly, and his demeanor changed in an instant. "I'm so sorry. I didn't mean to interfere..."

Sarah nearly dropped her soda bottle when she grasped what he meant. "No, no, no...we're not together. Just friends."

Her answer must have pleased him because he smiled and relaxed again. "Well, the movie should be ending soon, but I'll be here whenever you get ready to go."

Sarah thought about returning to the movie, but the images she'd seen earlier sent a chill up her spine. "Do I really have to go back in there?"

Doug laughed. "No, you can stay right here with me."

Sarah propped her elbows on the counter and leaned in as close as her pounding heart would allow. "I like that idea much better."

* * * *

Joseph glanced over his shoulder at Sarah and Doug, who were huddled together in a corner booth of the café while he sat at the counter near the entrance. He wasn't thrilled over what was happening, but there was little he could do about it. When he discovered Sarah talking to Doug at the concession stand at the movie theater, his first instinct was to get between them, but she was a grown woman and could take care of herself. (A fact she reminded him of daily).

As far as first impressions went, Doug seemed like a nice person, but he wasn't about to leave her alone with someone who was still practically a stranger. He promised to give them some space in the café, but he kept his eyes on them as much as he could.

"If I didn't know any better, I would think you were stalking them."

The soft feminine voice came from the barista behind the counter, but he could tell by her sly grin that she was joking with him – at least, he hoped she was. Joseph set his coffee down and awkwardly shuffled his feet on the tile floor. He couldn't decide if he was more embarrassed over being caught staring or the fact that he was caught staring by such a pretty woman.

"That's my best friend and her date. We're still kind of new here, so I probably am being a little overprotective."

The barista looked toward the corner booth and smiled. "I think it's sweet," she replied. "If it helps, I've known Doug a long time, and he's a good guy."

Joseph frowned. Actually, it didn't help. Although he'd never admit it to anyone, part of him hoped Doug would be a jerk and that Sarah would tell him to hit the road. Joseph looked their way again, and his heart ached when he noticed Sarah had moved closer to him in the booth and they were now side by side – literally. Doug whispered something in her ear that made her blush and Joseph turned back around in his seat. He didn't want to see anymore.

"You look like you could use something stronger than black coffee. How about a shot of Irish Cream syrup to go with that?"

Joseph was happy to oblige as he slid his cup over and watched her douse the steaming hot liquid with a generous dose of coffee syrup, something he never knew existed. When he took a sip, he nearly choked on the strong flavor, but it was good once he got past the first sip, and it did help him forget what was taking place on the opposite side of the café.

Joseph glanced at the barista's name tag clipped to her apron. "Thank you...Brittany."

She leaned over and rested her forearms on the counter and the faint scent of her feminine perfume ticked his nose. "You have me at a disadvantage."

He cocked an eyebrow and took another sip of his drink. "What do you mean?"

She gestured to his attire and laughed. "You're not wearing a name tag."

Joseph felt the heat rise to his neck as he put the cup down and held out a hand to her. "I'm sorry. My name is Joseph...Joseph Troyer."

She nodded and smiled before shaking his hand. "Well, it's nice meeting you, Joseph Troyer."

He didn't miss the flirty tone of her voice, and under any other normal circumstances he might have taken that as a cue and asked her out on a date, but his heart just wasn't in it. One thing he'd learned since taking part in Rumspringa was that English women were very assertive, but none of them made his heart race the way Sarah did.

"Are you Amish too?" she asked. "I can tell your friend is, but you dress nothing like the other Amish men I've seen around Dayton."

Joseph groaned as he looked down at his clothes. It wasn't the first someone had asked such a question, and he was honestly tired of trying to explain to outsiders about the rite of passage he and Sarah were taking part in. A handful of them understood but most just gave him a blank stare and could really care less.

"It's a long story," he replied.

He was caught off guard when Brittany put her hand in his and leaned in closer – so close that he could feel the warmth of her breath on his skin. "Why don't you tell me more about tomorrow night? During the fall months, there are different bands performing in the town square every Saturday night, and I'd love to see you again."

Joseph opened his mouth, but he didn't quite know what to say. He'd never had a woman ask him out on a date before. He glanced over his shoulder at the corner booth, and his heart plummeted to his feet when he saw Doug kiss Sarah's cheek. She blushed profusely, but the way she smiled at him made her whole face light up and she looked even more beautiful, if that was possible.

"That sounds like fun. What time should I pick you up?" he asked.

Brittany squeezed his hand. "I'll be working until 8:00, so why don't you just meet me here and we'll walk to the square? Is isn't far."

He knew he was probably making a big mistake, but...why not? He was tired of holding on to the hope that Sarah would someday see him as more than a friend, and it was blatantly obvious she was interested in Doug.

"That sounds like a good idea," he replied, a bit more solemnly than he intended.

A gentleman approached the counter with an order before she had the chance to reply, but she gave him a big smile before leaving his side to tend to her customer. He wanted to be happy – to be excited over their impending date – but he couldn't make himself feel something that just wasn't there.

"Hey, Joseph. Ready to go?"

The sound of Sarah's voice stole him from his reverie, and when he turned to find her and Doug standing behind him, he squared his shoulders and forced a smile. Doug had his arm around her shoulders and was holding her close, which felt like a dagger to the heart.

"Doug asked me to go with him to the town square tomorrow night," she mentioned. "There's supposed to be some band playing there."

His heart sank, but he thrust out his chin and summoned every bit of willpower he could to appear stronger and happier than he felt. "Brittany and I are going too."

He motioned toward Brittany, who finished up with her customer and came over to introduce herself to Sarah. They talked about the concert, and he hoped Sarah might be shocked or feel a bit of jealousy, but he detected nothing but excitement over their date.

"We should all meet here and go together," Doug suggested.

Joseph sat up straight. He didn't care for that idea at all. The last thing he wanted was to be subjected to more displays of affection between him and Sarah, but before he could object, Brittany was bouncing up and down and clapping her hands together.

"Yes! I love that idea!" she exclaimed.

And just like that, he and Sarah were thrown together on a double date, and there was no way he could get out of it without coming off like a jealous jerk. As the other three talked about which bands would be playing, Joseph slumped in his seat again and tried to tune out the conversation.

It was going to be a very long night.

* * * *

Sarah sat in the back seat of the taxi and tried to make small talk but Joseph continued staring out the window. The driver hummed along to a sad song on the radio, and the mood in the car was downright depressing. She thought back to their earlier conversations, trying to understand if she'd said something that may have upset him, but she was drawing a blank. When the taxi picked him up tonight, she expected him to be ecstatic over his date with Brittany, but he appeared just the opposite.

"Brittany seems like a nice person," she said. "Maybe, if things work out tonight, we can do something else together – just the four of us."

Still...nothing. Not even a grunt or a sideways glance in her direction.

"Joseph, seriously, what is wrong with you tonight?"

He finally acknowledged her, and even in the darkened confines of the car she could see the despondent look on his face. "I don't think that would be such a good idea."

She was taken aback by his comment, and at first, she didn't know how to respond. She thought they'd grown closer over the past two weeks while celebrating their independence, but maybe she was wrong. Perhaps he was tired of being stuck with her and wanted to do his own thing. She had to admit, the realization stung a bit.

"Have I done something to make you angry?" she asked. "You've barely spoken one word to me since last night."

Joseph slid over next to her so they could talk privately and not be overheard by the taxi driver. "I'm not mad at you, Sarah. I'm angry with myself."

She noticed the way he drummed his fingers on top of his leg, the way he always did when he was upset or agitated, and Sarah put her hand on top of his to try and calm him down. "Tell me what's wrong."

He seemed apprehensive at first, but it didn't take long before he opened up, and Sarah wasn't prepared for what she heard next.

"I hoped during our Rumspringa that I would finally be able to show you how I really feel about you, but I've been so nervous, and it looks like I may have lost my chance. I should've known someone would come along and steal you away from me. I've been such a coward."

He squeezed her hand and brought it to his mouth, and when he pressed his lips to the back of her hand, she felt a shiver race up her spine.

"I've dreamed of us being together for so long now, and I guess I took for granted that we would always be best friends and that no one would ever come between us. I should've known better. You are such a beautiful woman, and Doug or any other man would be very lucky to call you his own."

His confession stunned her, but not only did his declaration of love leave her blindsided, it sounded as if it was also meant as a goodbye, and that alarmed her even more.

"Joseph...I don't understand. Why haven't you told me this before?"

He shrugged his shoulders and looked out the window. "Like I said, I was a coward. I was afraid I might lose your friendship if you knew how I really felt about you, so I kept it buried deep in my heart. I regret that, but now you know. I just hope we can still be friends. I don't ever want to lose you."

Sarah felt hot tears stinging the corners of her eyes. He sounded so sad, and it was breaking her heart. The taxi driver announced their arrival as he pulled up in front of the café and Sarah spotted Brittany and Doug standing on the sidewalk.

Joseph squeezed her hand again.

"I love you, Sarah," he whispered.

He paid the driver and exited the vehicle before she had the chance to reply, and when Doug walked around to her side of the taxi and opened the door for her, she tried her best to smile and act as if nothing was wrong. He kissed her cheek and placed his hand against the small of her back and led her to the sidewalk. Brittany had already looped her arm through Joseph's and taken off in the direction of the town square and she and Doug walked quickly to catch up with them. The city was a bustle of activity and when they arrived at their destination, Sarah was surprised by the enormous crowd of people gathered around a gazebo and makeshift stage located in the center of the square.

It was so loud Sarah could barely hear a word Doug said, and when the band started playing, it tuned out his voice completely. Brittany and Joseph stood a few feet away from them and Sarah couldn't believe her eyes when she saw Brittany grab Joseph by the shirt collar and pull him toward her for a kiss. She tried not to stare but it was difficult not to. The move was bold – much bolder than anything she would ever dream of doing, especially with so many people around.

She saw Joseph put his hands on her shoulders and push her back, but it didn't seem to faze her. Between the band and the lively atmosphere, she was lost in her own little world, dancing around and waving her arms in the air. Joseph stood beside her and he swayed to the music, but he looked out of place – much like she felt.

Doug leaned in close to her ear. "I'll be right back!" he tried to yell over the music. She nodded and watched as he walked toward a group of men singing and dancing near the stage, but it didn't take long before someone jumped in her way and blocked her line of vision.

Sarah swayed to the music, but it was so loud she couldn't really get into it. She couldn't tell exactly what kind of music the band played. It was definitely nothing like she was used to hearing in church while she was growing up, and it was even weirder than the music the DJ played when she and Joseph went dancing.

Doug reappeared several minutes later, holding a plastic cup in each hand, and she thanked him when he gave her one. She hadn't eaten or drank anything since lunch and her mouth was parched. She'd hoped the four of them would eat before the concert, but apparently Brittany and Doug had other plans.

Sarah took a small sip of her drink, and she nearly hurled when it touched her lips and she realized it wasn't soda or water.

"What is this?" she asked.

Doug laughed. "It's beer!"

He seemed surprised by her question, but that didn't stop him from drinking, dancing, and carrying on with the band. Sarah, on the other hand, was speechless. She'd never drank alcohol before in her life, and she knew Doug wasn't old enough to buy it. The fact that he'd treated her to something illegal without a care in the world made her blood boil.

She was about to give him a piece of her mind when her path was suddenly obscured by blonde curls as Brittany hopped in front of her. "Is that beer? Can I have some?"

Sarah thrust the cup in her face. "You can have it all!"

Joseph gave her a skeptical look, but she didn't offer him an explanation, and the music continued for what seemed like forever. Sarah didn't want to spoil the party, so she did her best to ignore the way her stomach rumbled and the way her feet and legs ached from standing so long.

Doug and Brittany, however, seemed oblivious to everything except the music as they danced and yelled to every song. Doug left her side a few times to visit his "friends" near the stage and once he learned Brittany was interested, he brought back a cup for her each time. It didn't take long before they were both slurring their words and acting like fools. It was infuriating and embarrassing, to say the least.

"Let's go somewhere else!"

The sound of Joseph's voice startled her. She hadn't noticed him sneak up beside her, but she could detect his mood right away, and it matched her own. When he put his arm around her waist and started leading her toward the parking lot, she wasn't about to object. As far as she was concerned, they couldn't get away fast enough. Despite having to literally push their way through the crowd of people, they reached the parking lot relatively unscathed.

"So...what now?" Joseph asked.

Sarah crossed her arms over her chest and looked up and down the busy street. There were dozens of stores and restaurants on both sides, but she noticed a tiny diner about a block away, which she pointed to.

"I'm starving, and that restaurant looks like the farthest one from the square, so I say let's get something to eat."

Joseph nodded and laughed, and as they took off toward the diner, he grabbed her hand and held it, she assumed to keep from losing her in the crowd. Whatever his reasoning was, she didn't mind, because his secure grip felt oddly comforting to her rattled nerves.

The diner was empty except for the staff and one elderly couple, so they could pick any booth they wanted, and it didn't surprise her when Joseph led her toward the one in the corner, away from the front entrance and windows. The last thing they both needed was for Doug and Brittany to find them – not that they would be able to follow a straight line in their current condition.

Sarah slid in the booth while Joseph sat across from her. After they ordered their drinks and food, she leaned back in her seat and took a deep breath.

"It's been a long night, hasn't it?" he asked.

Sarah gave him a weary smile. "Do you think they'll be alright?"

Despite Doug being a jerk, she couldn't help but worry for his safety and Brittany's too.

"Brittany mentioned to me that they both live in an apartment complex a block from where they work, so they'll be fine. I just hope they sober up before they get arrested."

She shook her head and frowned. "That was the nastiest stuff I have ever tasted."

Joseph chuckled at her remark. "I'm sorry your date didn't work out like you hoped it would."

She wondered if he was telling the truth, especially after their conversation in the taxi, but she didn't question him. "I'm sorry yours didn't work out either."

He smiled at her. "Oh well, I guess we can chalk this one up as a learning experience."

The waitress appeared with their food and drinks and Sarah's mouth watered as she dove into her hamburger and French fries. The conversation flowed easily as they ate their meal, and it wasn't long before they were laughing off their doomed date situation and talking about more important matters.

"Have you made a decision?" she asked.

Joseph put down his glass and for a moment he was quiet as he contemplated his answer. "You mean have I made a decision to return home or stay among the English?"

Sarah wiped her mouth with a napkin and nodded. They hadn't discussed it since they ventured away from home, but it was always at the forefront of her mind since the very beginning.

"There are a lot of things I've enjoyed here, but it isn't near what I expected it to be, and I have to admit I've missed being home."

She felt the same way, and she was relieved when he said it first. The idea that she may have to return without him was something she couldn't bear, and she also couldn't stand the thought of telling his parents and younger sister he'd chosen a different path.

"What about you, Sarah? Do you plan on staying here?"

She could tell by the tone of his voice and the way drummed his fingers on top of the table that he was anxious over her answer.

"I know I complain a lot about working from daylight to dark on the farm," she began. "But I wouldn't have it any other way. I'm thankful for the values I've learned, and I honestly don't know what

I would do without my faith and the people we grew up with. I can't leave that."

He leaned over the table and took her hand in his, and a huge smile spread across his handsome face. For a moment neither of them spoke, and when he caressed her hands with the pads of his thumbs, she held her breath. His skin was rough from his many days plowing the fields, but his touch was hot and sent an unexpected rush of heat coursing through her body.

"Let's get out of here," he said.

It was the sweetest five words she'd heard in a long time, and her heart soared when she thought about how happy her family would be when she returned home for good. Her time in Dayton was an adventure she would never forget, but her heart wasn't in the English world, and it never would be.

They paid their tab and walked outside the diner, where they were greeted by the drizzling rain. Hopefully they would be able to find a taxi and make it home before the downpours started since neither of them brought an umbrella. The temperature had dropped somewhat, and she couldn't wait to get home to her warm house and bed.

Joseph took off his jacket and held it open for her, and the sweet gesture made her blush. When she slid her arms inside, she sighed contentedly as the warmth of it wrapped around her body like a hug. He took her hand and together they walked quickly down the sidewalk. Everyone else they met seemed in a hurry to beat the rain too, and when a young teenager came barreling toward them on his skateboard, Joseph grabbed Sarah around the waist and pulled her out of the way to keep her from getting hit.

It wasn't until the danger passed that she realized he was holding her tight against his body, and when he realized it too, he instantly loosened his grip. It was an awkward moment, but she was more surprised over the loneliness she felt once he released her. He took her hand and tried to lead her away, but Sarah stopped him, and for a long while they just looked at each other as people walked around them without giving them a second glance.

Sarah looked up and down the sidewalk and when she spotted a narrow alleyway between two of the buildings, she headed for it, pulling Joseph along behind her.

"What are you doing?" he asked.

Honestly, she didn't know, but she was suddenly overcome with an overwhelming need to be alone with him, and the alleyway seemed like the closest place to do that. It was all so spontaneous she didn't have time to work out the details, but as soon as they stepped inside, she panicked over what she would say to him.

The space between the two buildings couldn't have been more than four feet, and as they stood facing each other, she was very much aware of how close they were. Fortunately, the alleyway was deserted so they wouldn't be disturbed.

"Sarah, what's wrong?"

The sprinkling rain turned to heavy droplets, and Sarah knew she needed to do something before they were caught in a torrential downpour. "Say it again. What you told me in the taxi."

Her heart beat wildly inside her chest, and she was afraid she might be making a fool of herself, but as the confused look on Joseph's face melted away to recognition and a smile, she breathed a little easier. When he ran his fingertips along her jaw, Sarah felt her knees weaken.

"I love you, Sarah. I always have."

And there it was again – that strange sensation she felt earlier while they were standing on the sidewalk. It was a new and different emotion she couldn't describe, but she knew in her heart that she owed it to herself to see where it would take her.

"Kiss me," she murmured.

Joseph didn't hesitate, and when their lips touched, Sarah braced her hands against the brick wall behind her to keep from sliding into a puddle on the concrete. The kiss was brief but left her trembling.

"What are you thinking?" he whispered, while slipping his fingertips down the side of her neck. His touch was soft and soothing, but she could sense an urgency just beneath the surface.

"I don't know. I can't describe it. Perhaps you should kiss me again. Maybe that will help."

He laughed softly, and the deep rumble of his voice washed over her and made her heart race even faster. When he kissed her again, he didn't hold back, and as he pressed her body against the wall, she held on to him with every bit of strength she had left. When they separated, she was left breathless and weak and worried that her legs wouldn't keep her upright.

"And what about now? Can you describe it?" he whispered in her ear.

Sarah smiled. "Not really...but it's good. I promise."

A couple of raindrops fell on her cheeks and Joseph tenderly wiped them away before kissing her forehead. "Let's go home."

When he led her back to the sidewalk, Sarah felt genuinely excited for the first time in years. She was excited over new beginnings, the future, and the promises it held, but most of all, she was excited for home.

What a beautiful place to start.

REBECCA'S RUMSPRINGA

ALANA MILLER

Rebecca stared out of the window of her bedroom, the one she shared with her younger brothers and sisters. The fields rolled before her, barren now that the harvest was over. She had begged her parents to delay the Rumspringa, until after the harvest at least, even though her birthday had just passed this summer. She had tried to convince them to let her stay, but they insisted she go.

"Rebecca, would you come here please?" her mother called from the kitchen.

"Yes, Momma." She called back and deposited her knitting into the basket at the corner of her room. Rebecca fixed her skirts, brushing off yarn hairs that were attracted to the plain navy color. She walked down the hall and into the kitchen. Her mother pulled a fresh pie out of the oven and set it on a potholder on the table.

"Rebecca, can you go down into the cellar and fetch me another can of apples? Then go and fetch your siblings from the barn for supper."

"Yes, Momma." Rebecca said, and pulled on her boots. She stalked across the ground to the barn as the sun began to dip behind the hills and trees. She could hear her younger siblings screeching and laughing in the hayloft. She pulled open the door and smelled the sweet hay and manure.

"Come on, kids. Momma says its supper time." She called to the hayloft. She heard their muffled giggles and the boards sigh as they shifted their weight behind the hay bales.

"Alright, I guess I'll just have to eat all the potatoes and carrots from the roast Momma made. I know how much Anna and Naomi and Fannie love those little sweet carrots. Too bad they're not out here." Rebecca called and turn to leave. She heard her young siblings scramble down the ladder.

They raced past her into the house. She walked behind and lingered for a few more seconds, hoping to catch a glimpse of the neighbor boy, Joshua Hostetler. He was a cute boy, nearing manhood, and possibly looking a wife soon. She would catch him glancing at her when they were both working their respective fields with their families, or when they passed each other after services. Of course, she would glance back, but sparingly.

They sat around the dinner table, her father said the blessing, they ate. Rebecca's mind wandered as she picked absentmindedly at her plate. She wondered what she would see, who she would meet. She had heard about the outside world, how crass and improper it could be. She felt her stomach drop and twist with nerves.

Rebecca changed into her nightgown and sighed. She would miss her bed, the secret cat only the kids knew about who lived in the attic, the smell of hay.

"So, Rebecca, thought about anyone dreamy lately?" Anna laid sprawled across Rebecca's bed and flipped through the pages of her diary.

"Anna, you little snot!" Rebecca lunged and snatched the diary out of danger.

"What? It's fun to read." Anna slid into her own bed.

"That's rude, Anna! You're supposed to respect others and their feelings," Rebecca said, throwing her pillow at Anna.

"Well, if you marry Joshua Hostetler, then I can't marry his younger brother. When I come of age, of course," Anna said, brushing her hair back.

"You are too young to think about such things now. As the youngest, you'll have the worst choice anyways," Rebecca teased and brushed Anna's hair. Naomi, Fannie, and Maggie sit on the bed.

"Tells us about what you and Joshua," Naomi said. Rebecca smiled softly and started to braid Anna's hair.

"Me and Joshua will live in the old King house, that beautiful one with the large attic room and the big kitchen. We'll have so many children, eight or nine. I'll make quilts for all of them and have lots of grandchildren and be the best mother and wife and grandmother.

I can't imagine anything better than just being happy and in good health with a good husband." Rebecca said. Her mind wandered to her marriage day.

She said good night to her siblings and tucked them all into bed. She crept downstairs and watched her parents sleeping for just a moment. She crept back upstairs and knelt by her bed and said her prayers.

Dear God, please watch over my family. Thank you for giving me this day and thank you for giving me tomorrow. Please let my siblings grow up strong and let my parents grow old. Please let me bless my family with lots of children and grandchildren. Please bless all my sisters with good husbands and my brothers with good wives. Thank you for this good harvest and please let next year be just as good. In your name I pray, Amen.

She got into bed and began to write in her diary. The candle light fluttered and flickered as she wrote. She wrote about her day, about tending her mother's herb garden, about the socks she was darning. She wrote about Joshua, as well, just a little bit. Then she blew out the candle and snuggled under the thick handmade quilt.

Rebecca rose before the sun, just like every other day. She dressed quickly, pulling on warm thick socks against the cool fall. She crept down the stairs slowly. Her mother sat in the rocking chair by the front door. She grabbed her mother's shoulder.

"Are you ready to go?" They both looked out the window as the sun began to color the sky.

"Yes, Momma. I'm not sure if I really want to go," Rebecca said softly. Upstairs, she could hear tiny feet stirring as her brothers and sisters woke up.

"It'll be good for you. You need to see something other than the same old farm and same old people. You don't feel restless now, but you will if you don't take this opportunity. Go be young and free so you can come home and start a family and be a good wife," her mother said, squeezing Rebecca's hand.

"So you went on your own Rumspringa, then Momma?" Rebecca knelt by her mother's chair.

"Aye. It was actually a bit boring. I went up the road to the town and stayed with a very nice English family. It was summer, and I tended their children and their house while the parents were working. They were good Christian folks. It was refreshing to get out, and see how the world works outside. But I'm sure things have changed since then," her mother said, reminiscing.

"Do you want me to get you a gift while I'm out," Rebecca joked.

"Maybe just a new recipe or some new fabric for a quilt. I'm thinking something with purple or green in it."

"Alright, Momma. I'm going to go finish packing." She kissed her mother's hand and stood. Her siblings rushed down the stairs and into the kitchen. Rebecca walked back up the stairs and finished packing her knapsack; her diary, an extra dress, two extra pairs of socks, and an extra bootlace.

She said goodbye to family when the sun finally rose. She hugged her siblings tightly. Her father hugged her tighter and longer.

"I'll miss you, little flower" he muttered.

"I'll miss you, too, Poppa," she said back into his shoulder. She kissed her mother's cheek and hugged her tightly, too.

Then she set off. She hefted her knapsack onto her shoulder and set off down the old dirt road. As she passed the Hostetler farm, Joshua waved her down from his porch. He shouldered his own pack and jogged across the yard to the road.

"Hi, Rebecca. Mind if I walk with you?"

"Not at all. How are you, Joshua?" She shifted her bag.

"I'm doing well. Let me take that for you." He grabbed her knapsack and slung it over his other shoulder.

"Are you excited," she asked, putting her hands in her pockets.

"Yeah, a little. I want to go and see a movie and taste popcorn." Rebecca glanced at him, out of the corner of her eye. He was handsome, in his dark plain shirt. She didn't feel quite pretty enough standing next him in her plain black dress. She wanted him to notice her, but she didn't want to act like those English girls who wore too much rogue and too little clothing.

"That sounds fun," she remarked lightly. Her stomach fluttered with nervous butterflies.

"What do you plan on doing?" He looked straight at her now. *Straight and honest like a good Amish man,* she thought.

"I'm going to find some fabric for my mother, and maybe some toys for my siblings. My father didn't want anything, but I'm going to find him a new book."

"Rebecca, this is a chance at freedom, not a market trip," he laughed. She liked his laugh, deep and hearty.

"Aye, I know. But I don't really want to go on this trip to begin with, so I figured I would make it a practical trip," she sulked.

"You are a proper Amish woman, if there was ever one," he chuckled and adjusted their packs.

They met Sarah at the edge of the community. They stood for a moment under the gate. Rebecca rubbed her fingers together, trying to rub a little warmth back into them.

"Good morning, Sarah." Joshua said politely.

"Good morning, Joshua. Are we ready to go," she replied. She hefted her pack high onto her shoulder and set off down the road towards town.

"I guess we're going," Rebecca muttered. She and Sarah had been friends long ago, but when Sarah made her intention clear of leaving the community, their friendship faltered. Sarah had been shunned and Rebecca had not been allowed to even talk to her friend. Rebecca had wanted to be there, to help her friend through what must've been a hard time to come to the decision to leave the only community she knew.

They tromped down the road side by side. Cars zoomed by, some honked, some had teens leaning out windows and yelling at them. Someone even threw trash at them. Rebecca took Sarah's hand. She didn't take Joshua's. When they made it into town, the sun was high overhead. Between them, they had a little over $70.

"Do you know where we should go? Or what we're supposed to do?" Rebecca looked between Sarah and Joshua.

"We find a place called a hotel. We get a room for the night. Then tomorrow I'm going to the city. You two can do whatever," Sarah said disdainfully.

"What's in the city?" Joshua fixed a stern look at Sarah.

"A publishing house. I'm going to be a writer, a famous writer. I'll cut my hair short and wear pants." Sarah remarked. She shifted her bag and stalked off down the street. She glanced over her shoulder at Rebecca and Joshua, then ducked into a restaurant. Joshua looked at Rebecca and shrugged. They followed her down the sidewalk and into the restaurant. As they sat down at a table, Rebecca noticed the strange looks they garnered. The young waitress who took their orders gave them curious glances from across the restaurant. Her name tag said Helen. She was short and petite, with long blond wavy hair pulled back into a high ponytail.

"I'm sorry to stare, but you're Amish, right?" The waitress looked at them, with the same curiosity of a child seeing a lion at the zoo for the first time. She had a strange accent, drawing out some of the vowels.

"Yes, we're out on Rumspringa, which is like a journey Amish youth take before becoming full-fledged members of the community." Rebecca smiled sweetly at the girl.

"That's pretty cool. A lot of local kids just go to the big city for a couple months before coming back here. Some of them go to college and meet people, then come back and settle down. "

"What do they do in the big city?" Sarah said, her eyes shining brightly.

"Party usually. They just do stupid stuff and pretend that they're adults. It's boring, really." Helen shrugged.

"So, what do you local kids do?" Joshua said, giving the waitress a strange half-smile. Rebecca felt a strange thread of jealousy. *He's never given me a smile like that,* she thought. She considered pouting, but she was an adult now, she didn't need to pout.

"We go to the library and the movies and the mall in the next town over. Sometimes I hit up a barn party on the other side town. Just every now and then. It's kind of fun." Helen shrugged again.

After they ate, Sarah dragged Rebecca towards the back of the restaurant, towards Helen.

"Helen, right? I'm Sarah and this Rebecca. I was wondering, I don't want to impose, but do you know where there's a store nearby? I don't think we brought enough clothes and we just need to pick up something to blend in a little better."

"Oh, yeah. There's a place just a few doors down. If you want to wait just a little longer, I'll be off work and I can get my friends Alex and Tiffany to help us out. Alex loves shopping," She said, trailing off a little at the end.

"Oh, thank you, but on second thought, I think we can manage on our own," Rebecca stuttered nervously.

"Are you sure? I seriously don't mind," Helen said.

"Yes, we'll be fine. We don't need to impose on your charity," Rebecca said, more forceful now.

"Alright. I'm not very familiar with how things work out in the boonies up here, but I'm from the South. Besides racism and comfort food, we have hospitality. That means we take care of our guests." She took her apron and flung it on the counter.

"Delilah, I'm taking my lunch now!" Helen grabbed Sarah and Rebecca's wrists and dragged them out of the restaurant. Joshua scrambled after them. Helen pulled out, what Rebecca assumed was her phone, and tapped on the rectangular glass repeatedly.

"Alex, I need you to drop everything and meet us downtown now." She paused. "No, fashion emergency. And get Tiffany down here too." She paused again. "Yes, yes. I'll see you in a moment." She pushed the rectangle back into her pants pocket.

She pulled the two girls after her, down the smooth sidewalk. Joshua jogged to keep up with them. Helen pushed the two girls into a small corner shop that was mostly windows. The shop was packed with clothing racks that erupted fabric of all shapes, sizes, and colors. Even from all the stories and scant images, Rebecca could still barely believe all the colors and fabrics stretching before her.

Helen set about pulling article after article from the racks. A bored looking youth manned the counter. Rebecca couldn't tell much about the youth; they had short chopped up colored hair, and scary spikes through their eyebrows and ears. Rebecca was intimidated by them. But they made her feel overexposed; that typical English teen made her feel so out place. Joshua watched as Helen piled clothes on both of the girls. She then pushed them into tiny cubicles and closed the doors.

"Start trying those things on. I had to guess at a lot of your sizes, since those dresses don't do you girls any justice," Helen yelled and threw the piles over the top of the door.

Rebecca looked through everything. *How does anybody get anything done when they have to spend so much time picking out clothes and then putting them on,* she thought to herself as she stripped out of her dress. She picked up the first thing that caught her eye and glared at it. It was purple and strangely strappy. She couldn't decide if it was a sweater or a scarf.

"Helen? I think I need some help," Sarah called from her closet. Rebecca heard the chuckle from Helen.

"Luckily the cavalry has arrived, ladies," Helen chuckled and opened the door a crack.

"Rebecca, honey, this is Alex. She's going to help you get into those things. I didn't even think about the whole culture shock thing." Helen shoved a tall, slim girl into the changing room. The girl was dark skinned and had curly hair. Rebecca wanted to know how she got her hair to curl like that. Alex had a small gold stud piercing in the side of her nose.

"Hi, I'm Alex." She held out her hand to Rebecca. Rebecca took it and shook her hand like she had seen men do.

"Here, let me help you into that. Aren't you going to take that off?" Alex eyed the slip Rebecca wore.

"No? This is like our, uh, underwear." Rebecca blushed fiercely.

"Oh, okay. Then try this on instead." Alex handed her a bright blue sweater that Rebecca did like over the purple one. They spent hours cramming themselves into strange clothes. Rebecca felt like the English girls spoke a whole different language as they passed clothes back and forth to Sarah and Rebecca.

Size 4 instead of 6...

Grunge, not punk...

No, darker...

No, lighter...

Pastels...

More sparkles, Less sparkles...

At the end of the ordeal, Rebecca and Sarah muttered to each other and counted their money. The number crept higher and higher. Rebecca felt like her heart was going to explode and her stomach twisted in knots. They stepped up to the counter, ready to face the music. Helen pushed her way between them.

"Girls, put your damn money away right now." She slapped a plastic card on the counter top and glared over her shoulder at the two girls who clutched their money nervously.

"But, Helen –," Rebecca started.

"No. Away with it." The rectangle was swiped in the machine and the cashier bagged their clothes up. Joshua was leaning wearily against the wall. Rebecca picked up her bag of clothes. The plastic felt greasy and slick on her palm. Shame crept up her neck. As they exited the store, Rebecca wanted to turn and run.

"Thank you, Helen, for your generosity. We'll be on our way now." Rebecca looked down to avoid eye contact with Helen. Helen grabbed her shoulder.

"Let's go. My place is just a couple blocks away."

"Helen, we can't impose on you anymore," Joshua laid his hand over Helen's.

"It's not imposing. When you make new friends, you're supposed to take care of them. Tonight that means going to my house, sleeping in my beds, and eating my food." She winked at Joshua and squeezed Rebecca's arm gently. Alex pulled up to the curb in her car, a silver 4 door car.

They piled in; Helen sat in the front passenger seat and the other 4 into the back. Tiffany and Sarah sat squished against one door. Rebecca sat between the other door and Joshua. Joshua's leg pressed against hers snuggly. When they took corners too sharply, because Alex was not a very good driver, he would press harder against her. Rebecca could feel the heat in her face. She kept her eyes carefully fixed on studying the pattern of the back of the seat. Then he leaned over, on purpose.

"How do you feel about your first car ride," he whispered.

"It's a little hot and cramped. Do you think all car rides are this way?" He chuckled lowly in her ear. She could feel his breath on her neck. Her faced flared brilliant red as her thoughts began to race. *I wonder what it would feel like to kiss him at this moment...* She mentally chastised herself and sent a prayer to God, asking for forgiveness of her lust.

They stopped outside a two-story house. It was pastel yellow. There were large windows all across the front. Alex pulled into the driveway and parked. Rebecca fumbled with the door latch before finally squeezing it enough to open the door. She slid out of the car and onto the front lawn gracelessly. She straightened her skirts and brushed some wrinkles out. Her hands felt clammy and shook a little. She grabbed her old knapsack and her new plastic bag filled with new clothes.

"Your house is very large," Joshua observed. His eyes darted all around the house.

"Really? This is like a smaller house on this block. It's got like 3 bedrooms and only 1 bathroom. The back yard is a nice size though, good for a small or medium dog," Tiffany shrugged and walked up the stairs of the front porch.

"You lock the doors around here?" Rebecca stared at the chain of keys Tiffany picked through.

"Yeah? You don't?" Tiffany looked at Rebecca like she had just sprouted feathers. Rebecca had never needed to lock doors at home; they were a community and no one needed to steal anything.

They all pushed through the door. Sarah, Joshua, and Rebecca stood in the doorway, watching the three young women. Tiffany turned lights on all over the place. Rebecca played with one of the switches and watched the light flick on and off above her. Alex and Helen stand in the kitchen, tapping away on their phones.

"Okay, I'll get the girls set up in the spare bed. But where will we put sweet little Joshy?" Alex said and winked at Joshua. His face turned scarlet. Rebecca couldn't help but glare at her. Tiffany bumped her arm.

"Don't worry, she's teasing. She's very involved with her long-time boyfriend Thomas. They'll probably get married someday, but she's having too much fun being young," Tiffany whispered. She offered Rebecca a sweet smile. Rebecca and Sarah trudged up the stairs after Alex. She opened a door at the end of the hall, second door on the left, Rebecca noted.

"Sorry, there's only one bed. I hope that's not an issue." Alex glanced between the two girls.

"No, sisters share bed until one of the gets married." Sarah said and slid past Alex. Alex grabbed Rebecca's arm though.

"I saw your face downstairs. If I was out of line, I'm sorry. But if you would like, I can show you a thing or two about wooing a prospective male." Alex smiled sweetly down at Rebecca. Rebecca offered her an awkward half-smile and edged into the bedroom. They spread their new cloths out on the bed.

"These cloths are so weird. They don't feel... right," Rebecca said and ran her fingers across the clothes. Sarah shrugged and stripped out of her dress. She pulled on her new clothes quickly. Sarah looked in the mirror above the dresser and pulled off her prayer cap.

"I like them." Sarah left the room. Rebecca gaped at her. Then she stripped off her own clothes and pulled on the black slacks and baby blue sweater. She looked in the mirror too. She saw a young girl staring back, one who was afraid of her future. The stark white prayer cap covered her brown hair. She also removed the cap and her hair fell into a long braid down her back.

Rebecca walked down the stairs slowly. Her gut knotted when she thought of what Joshua would think of her. Only married couples saw a woman's hair. She walked into the kitchen, in only her sock covered feet. Sarah and Tiffany sat at the table, talking about her hair. Helen opened a rectangular box and Rebecca felt her stomach grumble.

"Here, this is the most American food that has ever existed. Pizza!" She held a slice covered in pepperoni out to her. Rebecca took a bite out of the cheesy triangle. The hot cheese burned her tongue but tasted amazing. She smiled and nodded at Helen's expectant face. But pizza was forgotten in a snap; Joshua walked in a plain white t-shirt and dark blue jeans. Rebecca's face flared again and she looked down, away from him.

"Rebecca..." He didn't finish that thought. The unspoken intimacy between them, felt by only them, created tension that pervaded the room. Alex cleared her throat loudly.

"So, there's a party going on tonight, if you guys want to hit it up? We can finish some pizza and get out there," Helen said, leaning heavily on the table.

"Yeah, let's go!" Sarah lit up.

"Okay, that's settled. Let's go get ready, ladies. Joshua, you look great already." Alex winked at him again and herded the girls up the stairs. Joshua's eyes never left Rebecca.

Upstairs, in Alex's bedroom, Sarah and Rebecca were subject to poking and prodding, being stuffed into strange tight dresses. Rebecca pulled on the strange tights under her short dress. They made her miss her thick, comfy socks. The English girls smeared her face with make-up; reddened her lips and lined her eyes in thick black lines. They pulled her hair and curled it and brushed it. Rebecca couldn't recognize herself after they were done with her.

She walked down the stairs holding onto Helen's arm. Joshua looked up at her from the bottom of the stairs. He looked a little disappointed, but he didn't take his eyes off her. Rebecca felt a small sliver of pride knowing that Joshua only had eyes for her. They piled into Alex's car and drove off to the party. Rebecca felt a little more comfortable this time, sitting next to Joshua. *I'm almost in his lap, What am I supposed to do if something like that happens?*

They walked up to the barn. Joshua was still taller than her in her ridiculous shoes that squeezed her toes and made her ankles feel weak. *Or maybe Joshua is why my ankles feel weak,* she thought to herself with a secret smile. Loud music pounded and Rebecca could feel it in her heart, like a second heartbeat. Inside, there were barely any lights. Rebecca could see teens dancing with each other; it looked like animals mating. She wanted to turn and leave. Helen pushed a plastic cup into her hand and demanded she drink it.

The alcohol burned her throat. She gagged and coughed. Joshua was whisked away into the party by several guys that Alex and Helen knew. Rebecca leaned against a wall and watched teens kiss and grind and drink. *This isn't the place for me...* Someone grabbed her arm and startled her.

"It's just me," Joshua screamed over the music. Rebecca smiled at him. He took her hand and led her outside.

"Sorry, I just needed some air. Are you having fun?" He looked her up and down. He smelled of alcohol.

"No, but this will be a story to tell my kids and grandchildren," she chuckled.

"Let's take a walk." He took her hand again and led her down road. They walked for a few minutes. Then Joshua slipped his hand over her rear. She pushed him away forcefully.

"Joshua!" Rebecca stared at Joshua, her heart pounded against her ribs. Her stomach churned from the alcohol.

"I'm sorry. This is just a, a misunderstanding!" He glanced around. Panic was setting in and shone in his eyes.

"What do you mean, a misunderstanding? You've brought me out here in the middle of the night and for what? To catch our death of cold? And you gave me that nasty poison, for what? To drag me down into the filth and sin with Sarah? And then you try to start something that I gave no intention of wanting!" Rebecca felt the panic rise in her throat.

"I'm sorry, Rebecca. I didn't mean to. It was a stupid dare from those English boys I was hanging out with. I just wanted a chance to be alone with you." Joshua looked down. Even in the dark, Rebecca saw the blush creep across his face.

"Why? If you had wanted to talk to me, you could've said so!" Rebecca yelled, exasperated.

"I just didn't know how to talk to you. And those English boys were trying to convince me to 'make my move' on you." Joshua shoved his hands in his pockets.

"Oh Joshua," Rebecca sighed. The cold was starting to chill her.

Rebecca held the coat tightly against her body. She felt so small at that moment. *God, please watch over me and Joshua for what we are about to do,* she prayed silently. She shivered slightly.

"Joshua, come on. Let's go. We can walk to town in just a few hours," Rebecca said, holding out her hand. Joshua took it, his large calloused hand enveloped her smaller one. Her heart pounded even harder now.

"You shouldn't be walking in those ridiculous shoes," he remarked. She was wearing ridiculous shoes. "But you do look nice tonight," he added. She blushed and looked away from him.

"Do you think we'll be okay, being out here on our own?" She left out the rest of her thought. *Do you think we'll okay without a chaperone?*

"I hope so, Rebecca. This has got to be the worst Rumspringa in the history of ever." Joshua squeezed her hand gently. She hoped her heart wouldn't jump out of her chest.

"The first Rumspringa was probably terrible," she said, with a chuckle," Because back then, the English lived just like us, so it was probably just boring to leave." She laughed.

"That is a very good point," he said back.

"Have you thought what you'll do when we get back?"

"Yeah. I'm going to apprentice under Miles Yoder and learn how to care for cattle and such. I think it would be easier to have livestock than to tend a field." She watched him out of the corner of her eye. She liked seeing his eyes sparkle and she could see the thoughts racing through his head. She had much of the same thoughts constantly racing through her head.

"Have you thought about who you would like to marry, someday," Rebecca said, trying to be casual, nonchalant.

"Yeah, just a passing thought or two. You?" He squeezed her hand again. She squeezed his back. Her feet started to hurt now and her fingers had started to burn from the cold.

"Yeah, every now and then." She said, looking at him. He stopped and looked at her. Their English clothes were dirty from tromping through the dark woods. She felt tired in ways she couldn't have imagined.

"Rebecca," he whispered. It wasn't a question or a statement. He said it like he just wanted to hear her name from his own two lips.

"Yes, Joshua?" She felt like there were swarms off bees in her belly, buzzing and fluttering.

"Who do you think about when you think about your future?" He stepped ever so slightly closer.

"You really want to know?" She smiled up at him. She loved his jaw, his grey-green eyes she could barely see in the dark, the way his hair curled and the shadow of facial hair that had begun to grow.

"Yes."

"Kiss me," she whispered. Her heart pounded so hard against her ribs. His hands crept under her coat, but stayed on her waist. He pulled her close. She slipped up onto tiptoes, trying to get closer faster. But her ridiculous shoes had other plans. She stumbled into him.

"Sorry, I don't know what I thinking." She giggled and rested her head on his shoulder.

"I do," he said. His rough fingers turned her chin up slightly. Her breath caught in her throat as he leaned forward ever so slightly. It felt like time stopped in that moment. Her heart beat once, twice and then his lips finally brushed against hers. It was so soft, so gentle, so short. *Again*, she thought.

"Again? You sure?" He joked.

"I didn't mean to say that out loud," she laughed and clutched his jacket," do you think we'll get in trouble? I don't think that was allowed."

"If nobody knows, then I think we'll be okay."

Joshua put his arms around her and hugged her tight. She hugged him back.

"When we get back, we'll have to do things proper. All the courtship traditions and such," Joshua said, "Do you think your father will allow me to marry you?"

"Probably. He thinks your father is a good man, and will give me over willingly. I do like how the English move through courtship. That Alex girl has been with her boyfriend for many years, but they didn't have to hide it or ask any permission of anyone. And they divorce all the time!" Rebecca shivered in her coat.

"I know! Imagine if any of the women did that at home! The shunning, the outrage," Joshua said dramatically.

"Imagine if we went through courtship like the English! Kissing on the first meeting, married by the third, having children by the time we were together three months, then splitting up by our first anniversary," Rebecca draped herself against Joshua. Her feet hurt in those shoes, but she knew if she took them off she would only be colder.

"We wouldn't split up. You're stuck with me now, Miss Fisher." Joshua stopped and looked at her again. "If you'll have me, that is." His eyes were full of hope.

"Are you asking me to marry you, Joshua Hostetler?" Rebecca was cold and hot all at once. Tonight had been such a strange night.

"Aye," he whispered. Her cold fingers grasped his.

"Then aye, I'll have you," She whispered back.

"Then let's get back to town and back home."

"First, another kiss?" she asked quietly.

"Of course, my dear," he replied softly. His lips brushed against hers so softly and gently. She didn't know if it had been the alcohol in her body or love, but she leaned further into it. The kiss edged from adorable and chaste to passionate and fiery. Rebecca understood why English girls kissed boys all the time; it felt hot and intense. She felt like time stopped around them. She no longer felt her cold fingers and cold toes. It was addictive to be so close to him, to be just the two of them in that moment. He pushed her away gently.

"I'm sorry. Forgive me, I acted improperly," She whispered. Shame flared across her face. She couldn't bring her eyes to meet his. He chuckled slightly.

"So did I. Let's get back to town, you're freezing." He kissed her forehead. He took her hand and led her back to town and to the warm beds waiting for them.

"Hey, Joshua, want to hear something really funny?" Rebecca pushed her face against his arm.

"Sure," he chuckled.

"I'm not wearing any underwear!" Rebecca giggled.

"Come on, you need to sober up." He wrapped an arm around her shoulder and they walked home.

The next day, they all stood outside the restaurant. Joshua held Rebecca's hand tightly. They had changed back into their Amish clothing, their normal clothing. Sarah looked so strange from when she had arrived just a few days earlier; she had shorn her long brown hair so short, into what Alex called a 'pixie' cut, and was wearing typical English clothing. Rebecca was sad to see her friend leave, but was happy she had found where she belonged. *Dear God, please watch Sarah as she walks a different path,* she prayed silently.

"Okay, you crazy kids. Be safe, don't fall off your horses and such. I'll be stopping by in the future to see your wedding, and oh- meeting your children!" Helen sobbed a little. Rebecca hugged her close.

"Aye, we'll be waiting for you. We'll send out invitations with all the dates and such. Amish have very intensive courtship traditions." Rebecca wiped a stray tear from her own face.

"I hope we're invited, too," Alex asked and hugged Rebecca tightly and then hugged Joshua tightly.

"Of course. Everyone will be invited. It'll be the biggest wedding, with Amish and English sitting down and celebrating our marriage," Joshua exclaimed and hugged Rebecca tightly. She couldn't help but giggle.

"Now get out of here! Go get to courting!" Helen sniffled and pushed them gently. They walked down the road, hand in hand. Their future was bright, and almost in their grasp. Just a few more steps down the road. Rebecca saw their lives playing out in front of them, the happiest in Joshua's face on their wedding day, the purity of the wedding night, the joy of their first year together and of their first child. On and on, their lives would be happy and peaceful. Rebecca was content to know that she was on her path and she had the man of her dreams next to her for every step of the journey.